Ordinary VICTIMS

LISA BRITTON BLAKELY

AND

DELRICK J. JOHNSON

ISBN 979-8-88862-129-5 (softcover)
ISBN 979-8-88862-130-1 (ebook)

Printed in the United States of America.

CONTENTS

CHARACTERS

The Main Character	David O'Brien
David's Parents	John & Rebecca O'Brien
David's Best Friend	Nelson Booker
David's Girlfriend	Daniella Sanchez
Daniella's Family	Ramon, Sr., Consuela & Ramon, Jr.
Daniella's Friend	Summer Knight
The Minister	Rev. Maurice English, Jr
Wife	Sarah English
The Teacher	Mr. Jayson Rochester
The Neighbors	Marsha & Krista
The Victim	Cherie Robinson Miller
Her Husband	Jacob Miller
The Survivor	Michelle Richards Greene
Survivor's Husband	Joshua Greene
The Counselor	Dr. James Watkins II
Wife	Lynne Watkins
The Store Detective	Michael Smith
His Wife	Whitney Springfield Smith

FOREWORD

Praise be to God from whom all blessings truly flow!!!

Thanks to all the victims and survivors with whom we have been allowed to have contact, friendships, confidence and love.

We all have a little victim within us. Some of our victims are blatant and observed by all; others are hidden deep within us where we suffer in silence. Some of us act on them and may end up in the legal system. The bottom line, however, is what we do with these; Do we remain that way? Do we overcome it? or Do we give it to God?

PREFACE

David's mind and heart were both cluttered as he listened and observed all the flurry of activity in the courtroom. Whispered discussions between attorneys; the tap, tap, tapping of the court reporter; the heavy thud of the rubber soled shoes of the court bailiffs and the swishing sounds of papers being shuffled only added to David's escalating anxiety. How had he ended up here? What would be the judge's decision? Where would the next few weeks, months or years of his life be spent?

CHAPTER ONE

The Decision

As the six-year old walked down the dusty roads of his quiet little sleepy hometown to the local neighborhood grocer, he felt the sharp, piercing pains of boredom. This was not the everyday, restless, wish there was something to do lethargy, but rather, it was abdomen burning, mind blowing, one hundred per cent bona fide BOREDOM. Then like a bolt of lightening, the idea struck him. The forming of this idea was to forever change the course of his life. As he sat behind the bars of his human cage years later, he would remember this very moment. The moment of clarity when the streets were quiet, the sun was brightly shining and how the sharp pains felt in the pit of his stomach.

When the scraping sound of the key turned on his freedom, David reflected on that moment. This led to a barrage of thoughts of how he ended up here. From his earliest memories, home was a place of pain—not the nurturing sanctuary of security that children need. This is actually what led to his search for comfort—initially via ministers and schoolteachers, but eventually through a more deviant lifestyle.

The bolt of lightening idea David experienced had to do with the fact that he felt invisible and insignificant to others. His thought was since he was invisible; he could use this to his advantage. Instead of being powerless, he would be powerful and invincible and he could do it without being caught since in the mind of a six-year old, he was "invisible". David now understood that sharp pain of boredom actually masked feelings of powerlessness, insignificance and a need to be noticed and valued. Yes, he had chosen the wrong way to fulfill this need, but at the age of six, he did not have the wisdom and maturity to know this.

As David walked down memory lane, he thought of his parents, their sacrifices and the hopes and dreams they had for him. Though he often viewed his home as being painful, he now had the hindsight to recognize it was not an environmental pain. His parents had been good to him: David had just been born with restlessness and a need to be in control of himself and his surroundings. This is very difficult for a child. The catalyst that had put the wheels of motion in place to result in David's present circumstances, however, began even before David's earliest memories could be formed.

CHAPTER TWO

The Parents

(John)

Watching the doctor smack his son on the bottom and listening to the lusty wail of the child, John O'Brien's heart swelled with pride. Hopes and dreams began spinning in his mind and John felt this was what really counted in life. He began imagining his son as a successful Black male who did not have to struggle as he had. His son would have the best; a home, an education, his own trucking business and no worries about how/when he would eat. John had hoped one day to own his own trucking business. He now added to that dream by thinking this was a business he could now pass down to his son.

(1973)

Feeling good and smiling broadly to himself, the five foot ten, brown eyed, muscular built, handsome twenty six year old African American male fingered his full beard as he felt his dreams were about to be realized. The youngest of three boys, John had always dreamed of following in his father's footsteps, as well as his grandfather's and great grandfather's, as an over the road truck driver. Almost all of the O'Brien males were truck drivers. He, however, wanted to go a step further and actually own his own trucking business. He had already financed this rig he was driving and had only twenty payments left. This trip had been successful enough, he might even be able to double some payments and still have some to place in savings.

As he was heading up the interstate towards his favorite truck stop in Oregon, John was looking forward to his usual meal of mashed potatoes and roast beef. The truck stop was notorious for its home cooked meals and the best apple pie in the Midwest. As he was progressing towards his destination, he made a mental note check in with his parents.

The sun was setting and settling into beautiful reds and oranges as the time was passing. John's stomach was growling and shoulders aching so he was ready for the much-needed rest. Pulling up into the parking area, John immediately checked in with his parents (via phone), washed in the restroom and settled into the corner booth. As he was mentally recounting the phone conversation with his mother, the unknown waitress suddenly diverted John's attention. He always ate here, but had never seen this vision of beauty previously. All former thought processes ceased!!! Coming toward him was a five foot two inch, shapely, red haired, red boned female who could only be described as "poetry in motion". John heard a sultry toned, honeyed voiced "May I get something for you?" Without thinking, he responded, "Yes, your phone number would be just fine". Taken off guard, yet oddly attracted to this stranger, twenty-one year old Rebecca Harlan gave a self-conscious giggle and asked if she could get him something "from the menu". John responded with "if this is my only choice". He ordered his meal, but took advantage of every opportunity speak with her and learn something about her. He prolonged his eating as long as possible, not wanting to leave without her phone number, but not wanting to come across too forcefully. At last, he had no more delays and Rebecca brought him his ticket. John sighed deeply, trying in vain to think of another way to get her phone number, when he noticed a smiley face and a ten-digit phone number at the bottom of his ticket. His heart soared, his eyes sparkled and his smiled broadened as he nodded at Rebecca and went to the register to settle his bill. He, also, decided to stay over in Oregon tonight instead of beginning his journey home to Tennessee.

(Rebecca)

Rebecca was reeling with excitement as John departed. She was not sure if he would call, but she was sure hoping. The day she had applied to work at this truck stop was one of the most depressing days of her life. She had not anticipated having to work such a job as an adult, but the town was so small and the opportunities so limited, she had decided this was her lot in life. At least she was able to learn about the rest of the world vicariously through others who stopped at this truck stop. Secretly, however, Rebecca had always hoped she would find her "knight in shining armor". She dreamt of him coming here sweeping her off her feet and then the two of them would marry, have a family and live happily ever after. Could John possibly be the one? Could he be her knight in shining armor? Her face flushed just thinking about him. How could she have such a reaction from such a brief interlude???? Later that night, the phone rang. Rebecca paused in her household chores and grabbed her chest. Barely able to breathe, she tried to convince herself it might not be John. On the third ring, her dad answered and called out "Becca".

Trying to slow her heart, Rebecca casually walked to the phone. "Hello?" she answered in a breathless tone. She then heard that deep, sexy voice of the stranger she met earlier. Rebecca almost became dizzy with excitement. "Girl, you sound so sexy over the phone", he said in his southern Tennessee drawl. Rebecca giggled lightly as she said to him "you're so silly". She could not believe she was this casual; yet intimate with someone she had just met. They talked well into the night and made plans to meet for breakfast the next day before he would have to leave for home.

(Early Courtship)

The next day, Rebecca dressed exceptionally careful. Her mother became suspicious when it took her two hours to get ready as opposed to her usual forty-five minutes to an hour. Rebecca confessed she had met a guy. Her mother smiled profusely, glad Rebecca was getting out, but hoping within, this would not be someone who would use her baby and go on about her way. She, thus, cautiously, warned her to remember he was "passing through" only. Rebecca tried to retain this thought mentally, but was unable to hold onto it emotionally. Within her heart of hearts, she knew this was not the end for John and herself. She, somehow, had an inner knowledge that she would be seeing much more of John.

Becky's favorite color was purple, but when not dressed in her uniform, she generally wore dark brown or black in order to not draw attention to herself. Despite her desire to meet her Prince Charming and get out of this town, she was too shy to deliberately draw attention to herself. She had no idea this was not necessary anyway, because she was so stunning in her simplicity, men noticed. Most did not approach her because they were "passing through" and felt she deserved "more than a part time boyfriend". After all, someone that good looking had to either be taken or be 'stuck up' or just would not be interested in a truck-driving bloke. Rebecca, thus, went without dates and many a man missed out on a golden opportunity to know her. Tonight, however, Rebecca wanted to be noticed. She wore what she thought was a modest shift with a red scarf and red shoes.

She had no idea how the simplicity of the dress simply complimented her natural curves and beauty. She did get some idea about this when John gasped, grabbed at his chest and shook his head from side to side when he saw her. Flushed from the fairly nonverbal compliment, Rebecca felt as if her insides would fall out from nerves, but as they sat at breakfast, they both forgot how each looked and began to delve into the lives of each other.

Before speaking too much, Rebecca (or Becky as John had already dubbed her), did note how handsome John looked in his freshly pressed jeans and black turtleneck. He had been really self-conscious since he did not have what he considered appropriate clothing for "courting". He, after all, had planned to only pass through this town after ending his work shift.

The couple talked incessantly at breakfast and neither could believe how comfortable they felt with each other. John found himself sharing his dreams of owning his own trucking business and Rebecca shared how she often daydreamed of leaving this little Oregon town. Minutes turned into hours before the couple knew it. As time drew to a time when they knew they needed to go to their respective places, both experienced the sharp stabs of pain often accompanied by loneliness. Neither wanted to leave, but both knew it was inevitable. They had only known each other for twenty-four hours, but felt it had been a lifetime. John and Rebecca reluctantly parted ways for the day. John had to get on the road and Rebecca needed to get home. The couple made plans to see each other again soon, as soon as John's job would permit. Though these plans were in the making, one would have thought they were making plans for a funeral based upon their sad countenances. Both, individually, could not believe the reaction he/she was experiencing over leaving a virtual stranger, but this was stronger than both of them.

Much to the relief of both, they did see each other often and were soon man and wife. As a six-year old, David did not know this information nor could he have comprehended it, even if he had known. Moreover, he had no idea or ability to understand, that in a few years, fate would step in and present him with a very similar circumstance to his own parents'.

(John)

As John looked at his newborn son, he remembered the many miles traveled to see Becky over the next few months. They had a whirlwind courtship, but both had known it was right from the beginning. He recalled how beautiful she looked and how he could not hold the tears back the day she walked down the aisle as his bride.

Becky believed in him when no one else did. Now she had given him the ultimate—a baby boy. He had to prove himself worthy of her love and this child. Maybe it was time to come off the road—maybe he could do local runs so as to be home and be the family man.

John flashed back to when they first married. After settling in John's Tennessee hometown, they found their first apartment. Their first apartment home was not much more than one room with a bed, a couch and table. But with Becky's ingenuous creativity, they had fun making it a home. Now three years later, residing in their own doublewide home and starting a family, John considered it was time to build a bigger home. His wife and child deserved this and more.

For the next five years, John worked really hard at trying to make ends meet and be the family man, too. Eventually, however, with building their three bedrooms, two and one half bath, 2300 square foot home, finances became tight. Rebecca even had to go to work and though this helped, they just found out she was pregnant again. They were excited and so was David, but John began to resign himself to returning to over the road. He, also thought it might be time to resume chasing his dream of owning his trucking business.

(Rebecca)

Exhausted from giving birth, Rebecca's mind had been reeling, also, with memories. She too recalled how they met and how she felt. John had been her knight in shining armor just as she had imagined. Even though the doctor had told her she might have difficulty conceiving or carrying another baby, she so desperately wanted to make sure David had a sibling. Rebecca would not have survived her childhood without her little sister to love. They had each other even when their parents were working too hard to be with them.

Five years later, there were other memories to surface. At that time, Rebecca found her blessed second pregnancy was difficult. She indeed had problems conceiving, but finally, she had a positive pregnancy test. Her only concern was, due to financial responsibilities mounting, she was going to need to go to work after the birth of the baby. John was already talking about returning to over the road. This was reminiscent of her parents having to work all the time, but she felt good knowing she would at least be able to give David a companion even if they (the parents) could not always be there for him.

Going to work though was a problem she need not concern her with right now. Right now, she took joy in being pregnant again, having a loving husband and nothing compared to the excitement on David's face when he would feel his baby brother kick in her stomach. He would spend hours with her, asking questions and asking her to teach him to read so he could read to his baby brother when he was born. Plans were being made for David and the baby to share the bathroom between their rooms once it was established via ultrasound that the baby indeed was a boy. David was overjoyed at someone to roughhouse with and to have someone who would look up to him.

As the pregnancy neared full term, Rebecca began to experience unidentifiable cramping. One night when she found her gown soaked in blood, John had to rush her to the hospital. Rebecca prayed and prayed she would not lose this baby, but her prayers were not answered, as she desired.

Later, in life, she would recognize blessing in having only one child, but right now, she was devastated and could not fathom how to tell David. In addition to this, developing tumors were found in her uterus and the doctor said he needed to do an immediate hysterectomy.

(JOHN)

John and Rebecca could not believe this destruction of their fairy tale dreams. David, so very young, kept asking unanswerable questions about why God took his baby brother. Not knowing how to deal with his grief, John was more determined than ever to go back over the road and Rebecca began to sink into a deep depression. With John spending more time on the road, Rebecca felt even more pain and estrangement. Unwittingly, in their desire to protect David, they were hurting him. They did not have as much emotional time to give him and were so steeped in their individual pain and grief, it was several weeks before they noticed how withdrawn and quiet David had become. Rebecca, however, being a mom at heart, began to realize how long it had been since she had cuddled and talked to David. She, thus, pulled herself together, went to a doctor for a brief trial run of mild anti-depressants and recovered from her depression. What she could not know at that time, was the seed of discontent and the feeling of being invisible had taken deep root in David's mind and soul.

That very lusty cry John had felt such pride about when David was born was really just the beginning of events that led to David's memories and then to his current situation.

CHAPTER THREE

David

As the memories continued to scroll for David, he did not know of the happier times his parents spent. He did not know how excited they had been about his birth. He did remember an air of joy when his mother was pregnant, but then one awful night he was told there would not be a baby brother after all—God had taken him to live with Him.

Not understanding why his parents were so sad. David began to "act out" and tried to get attention from them. Was it something he had done? Was he the reason his little brother had to go to Heaven? Being too young to discuss this, David became disruptive and oppositional. He refused to do anything asked of him. He would scream and yell over the least little thing. David would throw his food on the floor, deliberately mess up his room and leave the door open for mom to see. When his mom would finally began disciplining him, he would simply stare at her, unconcerned, as if he did not know why she was yelling. David would run out the door and hide behind trees or in the garage and just laugh when he heard his mother calling for him. His tantrums grew and his mother became more disgruntled. Until she sought help for her depression, however, her responses were not consistent. Sometimes she would ignore him; sometimes she would yell; sometimes she would spank him. This only served to further frustrate David and cause his behavior to get more erratic. After treatment, Mrs. O'Brien became aware of how inconsistent she had been with David. She felt very guilty, but tried to make up for it in the future by being more steadfast and consistent in her discipline. It did help some, but so much time had passed, David was already on a path of destruction.

This prompted his memory of times when he had been allowed to do short over the road trips with his dad. This, of course, was before he had to enter school. David recalled seeing the road stretch far, far ahead of him and his father and how after there was no baby, his dad seemed sadder. David looked over at his dad's sad face and wondered if he was thinking about the baby. In his child like manner, he asked his father, "Daddy, was God mad at me? Is that why he took my baby brother to live with him?" His father had looked shocked and pulled the big rig over to the side of the road. He pulled David into a big embrace and assured him God was not mad at him. He said "Son, God loves you and so do your mom and me; we are very, very happy we have you as our special angel". That was the last memory David had of not feeling invisible to the world. Thinking of this now David, too, remembered his undisciplined behavior. What he was too immature to know then, he now realized if he had simply had this conversation with his dad earlier on, some of his decisions may not have had such disastrous consequences.

David was unaware that even as these memories were scrolling for him, they were for his parents, too. In fact, John was remembering that same incident and again, after all of those years, felt a stab of guilt. He, in his way of withdrawing to deal with his grief, had done a disservice to David. He was wondering if he had paid more attention, stayed off the road, been more supportive to Rebecca and had realized the profound impact this must have had on David, if they would be sitting here now.

(The Early Years)

Even as a toddler, David had the choleric need to control his environment. He needed to feel powerful and have people admire him. David had a penchant for choosing activities that had the element of the thrill of defying danger. He was and always had been his own person. He always insisted on being called by his proper birth name—not a nickname. When he was as young as two, his grandmother used to try to call him Davie, or Little David or even Dave, but David would have no part of it—he would stamp his little feet and say "I ees David!!!

(Rebecca)

Even as David was remembering many of the incidences in his life, his mother, too, was having her own memories. She, like David, was trying to figure out how her baby ended up here in this place. She and John had loved him so much. Rebecca felt such guilt about having had to work and spend so much time away from David. She knew this trouble he had gotten into, had to be her fault. John had to travel so much, it was really her responsibility to be mother and dad to David, and she had failed. Rebecca began remembering some of the earliest incidents with David. Even as a toddler, he was very independent and curious. How could she have let her precious baby get so out of control?

When David was about two, she remembered the times he would stamp his feet and insist on being called "David". She recalled when he would try to get his own cereal if she was not moving fast enough. One particular time when John had been away and she was busy getting ready for work, David wanted his breakfast right then. He was pitching tantrums and making demands to eat. Rebecca had asked David to wait, but he had run to the kitchen and grabbed the milk out of the refrigerator, nearly dropping it. Rebecca had been so flustered, she had yelled and asked him if he wanted a spanking. David, with big round eyes and serious expression had responded with "No, I just want some cereal!" Even now this brought a wry smile to Rebecca's mouth.

When David was even younger than two he would give these serious, yet blank expressions as the adults were gathered around yakking. One Thanksgiving, her parents, John's brother, Marcus, as well as she and John had all been ooohing and aaahing about David crawling. At the age of about seven months old, David sat up and stared at them as if they were ridiculous looking and ridiculous acting. His Uncle Marcus had called him "Dufus", which both tickled and irritated Rebecca. David, however, just continued to stare at them as if he was the adult and they the children.

Yet, another time bombarded her memory. This time, they had been at her mother's home. David must have been about three. He had gone into the bathroom and locked himself in. Initially, he had screamed for her to get him out, but fairly soon, he began talking calmly to her, as if trying to comfort her. Rebecca, not very mechanically inclined, had been struggling with getting the knob off the door. David would occasionally yell out to her that he could see her or ask her to send him some toys, etc. Rebecca had thought it strange that a three-year-old was so calm. Eventually, she had gotten the knob off and was able to see in the bathroom. It was then she noticed David stark naked, playing in the toilet and yelling encouraging words to her without even looking up. That should have been a red flag to her that David was an unusually adult like child. She should have realized this would lead to early boredom and possibly lead him into trouble. Why had she been so oblivious?? Now here she sat, waiting for a judge to pass down a sentence on her precious baby's life.

CHAPTER FOUR

The Beginning

As the idea began to crystallize, David arrived at the store. He wanted to test out his newfound idea. Maybe he really was invisible. He would know any minute now. He picked up the milk and bread he had come for and in the process, slipped a candy bar in each pants pocket. He then sauntered to the register to pay for the milk and bread. His heart pounded so hard he just knew the cashier would hear him, but all he asked for was the money for the items on the counter. The excitement rushed to David's head and heart, as he walked out the door, with the cashier none the wiser. This must have meant David could act invisible when he needed to be. As he got a block from the store and there was no one chasing him or yelling for him, he took out one of his prize candy bars and began munching. He could barely wait to have another opportunity to go back to the store and see what else he could get. The six-year old felt powerful, invincible and six feet tall. All feelings of boredom left as he began thinking of other ideas. As soon as he got home, he rushed to his room, hid the other candy bar and rested his head on his arms as he reclined on the bed, fantasizing about his new life of invisibility and power. This was the beginning of bigger things to come.

From that point on, David continually engaged in juvenile petty crimes and/or pranks. Some were all in fun; some were more dangerous. David began most of this alone until he met Nelson.

(Nelson & David)

When David, met Nelson, he found a way to fulfill his choleric needs. Not only would Nelson become his partner in his escapades, but he also gave his full devotion, loyalty and admiration to David.

Nelson and David met at school. Nelson was the perfect candidate to be David's protégé. Wearing thick-lensed glasses, walking slew footed and having some learning disabilities, the light brown skinned Nelson was immediately drawn to David. He admired him and the confidence he portrayed. David was not afraid of anyone—not the other kids nor the teachers. The other kids never made fun of David and when Nelson was with him, they acted as if they feared him, too. He felt as if David was his 'bodyguard'.

Often, Nelson talked in the third person to refer to himself. This was one of the reasons the kids made fun of him. David, however, did not see fit to taunt him. He actually felt some sympathy for him. Yes, he loved the way Nelson would follow him and seek his approval, but he was also his protector from the cruelties of the other children. Because of this habit of speaking in third person and his physical appearance, the other children would often shun Nelson if they were not making fun of him. David, though, took him under his wing. Though this attraction to Nelson seemed to be purely self-serving on the surface, David actually had the genuine emotion of compassion for Nelson. Even though he would not let his grandmother or others call him Davie, he would only smile when Nelson called him by that name!!!!

Because he was sometimes treated cruelly and he was an only child, Nelson really loved and appreciated the attention he received from David. In addition to being an only child, Nelson did not even have the privilege of being the only child and living with his parents—his father abandoned him at his birth when he learned of the disabilities. His mother passed away when Nelson was still a tot. Ironically, she was at the funeral of her aunt when she herself had a massive heart attack and died. Poor Nelson was left to live with his grandmother who was aging and did not have a lot of energy for an exuberant, special needs child.

Initially, the thrill seeking escapades in which David engaged and later involved Nelson, were childish antics (minor shoplifting childish pranks, etc.) Eventually, however, they began pushing the boundaries. David did not know then that these 'fun tricks' would eventually lead him on the roller coaster of events that would become more serious and more dangerous.

This thought triggered memories of when David's favorite paternal uncle would visit. His dad's brother was a pharmaceutical rep and occasionally would stop by their home while on the road. One weekend night when Nelson was spending the night, his uncle came to town. He had planned to visit with David's grandparents, but learned they had gone on a senior citizen's club weekend trip to a nearby casino. He, thus, decided to spend the night with David's family.

Uncle Marcus was so cool. He always had money, gifts and funny stories for David. David wished he could see him more than two or three times a year. His uncle was like a movie star. He wore cool clothes, drove a white Corvette, wore his permed hair in a ponytail and usually had a cigarette in his mouth. To David, at the age of ten, this was the ultimate in suave and sophistication. Uncle Marcus engaged in horseplay with the boys before talking to the adults. He always put the kids first and David loved this. When it was time for Uncle Marcus to spend time with David's parents, he told David to go to his room and get his gift of the new Snoop Doggy Dog's CD, "Doggie Style". The boys, happily, rushed off to the guest bedroom to acquire the new CD. Again, David thought "how cool" his uncle was. His parents would never have thought of this type of gift. His father usually brought him tee shirts, baseball caps, some kind of state souvenir or candy when he would come home from his over the road travels. While retrieving the CD, the boys came across some Newport cigarettes and much more.

Meanwhile, Rebecca was expressing how concerned she was that David's only friend seemed to be Nelson. She told Marcus she really liked Nelson, but occasionally wondered if this put too much responsibility on David. She noticed David tended to parent and protect little Nelson and she thought he needed a peer more on his level. Both Marcus and John (who also was home that weekend) dismissed these concerns as unfounded. They suggested it helped David to have some responsibility and John even pointed out that Nelson was company for David since they (his parents) were often too busy. This brought up the guilt Rebecca still felt about her miscarriage, never giving David a baby sibling and having to work a rotating shift that often took her away from home at night. They discussed this at length, with the men having a counterattack response for every concern David's mother had. She finally acquiesced that she probably was anxious for nothing. Had the three of them known what the two boys were up to even as they were discussing them, this conversation may have taken a different turn.

After David and Nelson had gone through Uncle Marcus's possessions as he had told them to, they had found the CD and more. They found cigarettes and cocaine. David knew exactly what the cocaine was because they were doing the DARE (drug abuse resistance education) segment in school this week. Nelson knew all about it, as well, because his class had been at the DARE program, too. They had seen videos on what the drugs looked like, what harm they did and were warned to stay away from them. Police officers had come to the school and talked all about the drugs. David really had listened, but seeing a real bag of the stuff in front of him, he, of course, could not resist testing it for himself. Nelson did not have as clear of an understanding, but knew it was supposed to be bad. He was curious too, though and wanted to be "just like Davie".

David and Nelson went to the back of the garage and lit the cigarette first. As would be expected they choked and sputtered as they tried to puff the cigarette like Uncle Marcus. They both found this amazingly funny. Next, they took out some of the cocaine. Nelson hesitated a little, but with his trusting heart towards David, he was willing to try it, too. The boys put some of it on their tongues, but suddenly Nelson fell to the ground and started jerking around uncontrollably. His eyes rolled to the back of his head and foam began dribbling from his mouth. David was so frightened, he spit out what he had in his mouth and ran to Nelson, saying, "please don't die, Nelson. Please don't die. You are my only friend and I love you little buddy". He was holding his own chest and rocking as he pleaded. The jerking stopped and Nelson slightly opened one eye while he had a smug grin on his face. David just stared in disbelief—what was going on?? Suddenly Nelson laughed and said "Nelson not die; Nelson just high. Nelson is funning with Davie". David did not know whether to hit or hug Nelson, he was so relieved. Then it dawned on him; he had seen Nelson foaming. What had caused this? When he inquired of Nelson, Nelson admitted he had alka seltzer tablets in his mouth. Since he often had digestive problems, his grandmother insisted he take the alka seltzer with him all the time. While David had been testing the cocaine, Nelson had slipped one of the alka seltzers out of his pocket and into his mouth. David had to admit Nelson got him and it was funny. He filed this in the back of his mind as a potential scam the two of them could use in the future. Overall, no harm was done this time and the boys slipped back into the house into David's room with the adults none the wiser. Despite the experimenting, David never tried cocaine again. The joke Nelson played was enough to keep him from even considering such a feat. Besides, David wanted to always be in control and even at this age, he realized using drugs could remove some of his control.

As David recalled this incident, he was actually able to surface from his dark thoughts and regrets and chuckle. Thinking of Nelson, regardless of his part in David being here, made him chuckle. Yes, many persons made fun of Nelson and most did not understand their relationship. Nelson, nevertheless, was truly David's friend. He was actually his only true friend and had remained so from the time they met over ten years ago.

David began reviewing many of the times he spent with Nelson and how Nelson was the one person he really believed loved and looked up to him. David believed his current girlfriend cared for him, but it was nothing like the love from Nelson. This caused David to think about his relationship with Nelson and his girlfriend. When he first became involved with his girl, he was really worried about how to interface the two relationships. He did not want to let her out of his life, but he was not willing to sacrifice Nelson for her either. He remembered the day clearly.

Nelson had come over to his house after school as usual. He and David had planned to "hang out". As was often the case Nelson wanted to go to the Arcade. Actually, David had already anticipated this and so had asked his girl to "meet him there". As they were headed for the Arcade, David told Nelson there would be a girl there he had seen before, but this time she was going to join them. Nelson was not overly thrilled because he wanted to spend time alone with his special friend, Davie. The other kids were not always nice to him and as Nelson got older and older, he became more and more aware of how mistreated he was. He, therefore, was very hesitant and asked David, "does this mean Davie not play with me anymore?" David assured him this was not the case; he just wanted his two good friends to like each other. He had told Nelson he now had a best "bud" and a best female friend. Nelson was still somewhat leery, but when they arrived at the Arcade, Nelson saw who it was and all seemed right with the world. The only other challenge had been to not hurt Nelson's feelings when David wanted to be alone with his girlfriend. Somehow, some way, it all worked out. David was hopeful if he should have to spend too much time locked up, his "best bud" and his "girlfriend" would stand by him and keep each other company, too.

(David)

Memories continued to cross the screen of David's mind. Though he and Nelson had engaged in numerous mischievous misdeeds over the years, most were David's creations. Nelson generally "went along with it" for the thrill of what he perceived as innocent fun and out of loyalty and love for David.

Before Nelson was ever on the scene, however, David remembered many of his individual antics. The prompting and desire to engage in such behaviors had to be something that was inborn and unharnessed within him. He remembered doing and thinking things even as a preschooler that he now wondered if other preschoolers thought or did. He never meant any harm by his behavior; he just desired some control, excitement and acknowledgement. Being chronologically older and even older emotionally, realized how others must have viewed him as very precocious.

Suddenly as if blinded by a bright light David clearly recalled being potty trained. He vividly remembered how easy it had been for he had loved being able to determine when he would go to the bathroom. He, also, remembered the feeling of constantly being admired and exuberantly praised by the adults for going to the bathroom by himself. Feeling some guilt, he remembered his cousin, Jeremy. Jeremy was the same age as David and would often come to the house. Jeremy, however, was not trained as early or as quickly as David. David recalled feeling what could only be described as disdain for this cousin when he still wore diapers. David's mother had once insisted Jeremy should spend the night with David and she had said he could wear some of David's clothes. David had been furious, stamping his feet and declaring "No, Jeremy is a baby; he peed his pants. He will peed my bed; No, he not wear my clothes!! Jeremy had just stared wide-eyed at David and David's mom had put him in time out for being rude and callous. David had not cared one iota. It did not change his mind, but since he was too little to fight, he did what he was told. He knew in that moment that he had to "hurry and get big" so he could rule.

Despite his little controlling, bossy attitude and behavior, David had always loved his paternal grandmother to pieces, (his maternal grandparents lived so far away, he had little contact with them) He had called her "gandmommy" because he could not say the "r" sound. His gandmommy was the only one who he would let treat him like a baby. He liked it when she babied him. He used to pretend he could not do things, like go to the bathroom alone or take off his shirt, just so she would help. Once when she was at his home, he needed to use the bathroom. Instead of going as always, he had rocked from foot to foot, yelling, "come on gandmommy, gotta go, gotta go! Hurry, Hurry!" he would insist until she had taken him. He, in his older, wiser years, wondered if this was because his grandmother babied him in a way that did not make him feel vulnerable. In addition, he wondered if maybe he acted babyish with her because he got what he wanted/needed when he wanted it and this gave him a sense of power.

As David grew older, he had continued his petty thievery. He had sudden insight that maybe the old grocery store owner actually knew what he was doing and had simply allowed it for some reason. Even now this angered David, but he realized as often as he had stolen, it had always been too easy. David shook his head and decided, no he could not know, he had to have just been good enough to get away.

The scroll of his thoughts moved forward and David thought of when he was in junior high. Before meeting his girlfriend, David and Nelson had committed many pranks. Most of these pranks included the torture of a timid science teacher. With this teacher, they had done things as releasing air from his car tires, placing blocks behind the tires so he would not know his car was actually on blocks and placing clear glue in his seat. They, also, put black shoe polish on the board erasers and of course, made indiscernible rude body noises. They sent love letters from what they said was a secret admirer. Once, they had even sent flowers to the teacher for him to get during class and had signed them as the secret admirer. They tortured him endlessly because they could. They always pushed it to the limits, but did not cross the boundaries that would get them identified as the instigators or get them in trouble.

David actually giggled to himself a few times as he thought of some of the pranks they had pulled. He realized now how cruel and childish some of the pranks were, even though he did not really mean any harm. He had just wanted to feel a sense of control and have some excitement in his life. David had much difficulty controlling his giggling as he thought of one Halloween prank Nelson and a couple of guys he had recruited to help them pull one year.

Every year for Halloween, the small town in which he lived, had a hayride for the young people. The first couple of times, this had been fun, but David had quickly become bored with it. One year, when he was eleven or twelve, he had come up with a great idea. He remembered the ghost tale that a man who was hanged in the eighteen hundreds from the main bridge in town. It was said if you went to the area late at night, when all was quiet and called him, you could see him falling off the bridge. David thought Halloween would be perfect for this. He and his crew had gotten the prank together, with the help of an older relative.

This particular Halloween night, he knew the older guy would be driving the wagon. As they got near the old bridge, he slowed down, saying the horse did not want to move. He began asking the kids if maybe it was a ghost there since sometimes animals could see ghosts that people could not. The kids began yelling and squealing with laughter though they huddled closer together in case this was true. Just as the horses began moving forward and were directly under the bridge, a man lunged from the bridge and fell right in front of them. Kids and chaperoning adults alike, screamed. A few of the teens jumped off the wagon and ran down the street. One of the younger girls fell off the wagon and got hurt. One of the chaperones actually passed out and had to be taken to the emergency room. David and Nelson had laughed themselves silly, but much of the town did not think it funny, especially since some of the people had run and others had gotten hurt.

Thinking back on this, David realized it may have been dangerous, but he, at the time, simply found it fun. He and his crew had rigged up a man by creating a head and then stuffing some men's clothes, wrapping a rope around the head, both to hold it on and to make it appear he had jumped. There had been two guys hiding on the bridge and their cue was when the wagon would stop to prepare the rigged up man for jumping. When they heard the horse move forward, they were also watching to make sure the dummy fell behind the horses so as to not scare them. It had worked perfectly in their young minds, but so many people were so scared and upset, they had canceled having the annual hayride from that point forward. David thought this was silly and he realized, even as he was giggling, that they had never revealed their responsibility in the prank. There had been an investigation by the local authorities, but they were never found out. He shrugged to himself and thought it had not really hurt anyone. Those who fell off of the wagon only hurt their shoulders and the older persons were only scared—nothing physical was really wrong. Those teens that had run off only got lost and had to walk home. Even now, in his mind, he felt nothing was really wrong with this prank and it had been fun for him and Nelson.

David could not believe how his life was flashing before him so swiftly in these few moments of time. He was only sixteen, yet he felt as if he had lived a thousand years. He, not only had memories of those close to him, such as Nelson and his parents, but he was remembering one time incidents. He was recalling people he had only met or observed briefly. Why was his mind being bombarded and flooded with this? He did not know, but the memories continued to flow.

CHAPTER FIVE

The Minister

Because of the difficulty of his life, David was emotionally years beyond his chronological age. He was searching for some meaning for his life even at this tender age of ten. Semi-perched on the hard church pews next to his mother, David found himself enthralled with the obviously spiritual man of God expounding on scripture. For the first time, he really listened to the minister and found his heart and conscience were pricked. He, with a look of admiration on his face, began to imagine what it must be like to be "The Minister". He would bet this man never got in trouble; always knew the right thing to do in every situation. He bet Reverend English, Jr. must have had the perfect childhood and now had the perfect life with his lovely wife and his six children. Why they lived in one of the nicest homes in the town, had a large flourishing church and all of Reverend English's children were either successful in their business or studying for degrees in college. Reverend English must have been God's right hand man.

As Reverend English entered his home study after service that morning, he felt the sermon had gone well. He knew he should be praising God and feeling grateful and fulfilled—yet there seemed to be an emptiness in him. He was willing himself to avoid temptation and not even look at the computer screen with the chat line as it was beckoning him. He had a loving, faithful wife, a beautiful home, children of whom he could be proud and a thriving church. He fell to his knees and ruminated over & over why, why, why did he feel so empty??? At that moment, he heard it—the light beep of the computer—the beep, which told him he had a message on the chat line.

Contemplating on how to respond to the beeping, Reverend Maurice English, Jr. was transported in his mind's eye to his childhood. He was no longer the minister the community knew, loved and respected; rather, he was a scrawny, scared wide-eyed twelve year old listening to the sounds of his mom being slapped.

Maurice, the youngest of five boys, was born to Reverend and Mrs. Maurice English, Sr. He always wondered why he was his father's namesake and if this was the paving of the way for him to become a minister as well. Maurice remembered the community loving and envying his father and their family. They, too, had the big house in the community and his father was the most eloquent speaker Maurice had ever heard. When Reverend Maurice English, Sr. expounded the word of God, grown men would fall to their knees, blubbering like babies. His father was considered a pillar of society; yet, in private, Maurice often heard the cries of his mother after hearing her body slam against the wall.

By age twelve, Maurice not only knew of the abuse his mother suffered at his father's hand, but he knew why. His father, the upstanding, righteous Reverend Maurice English, Sr., had secret affairs and his mother knew. These affairs were not only with strangers, but also with his church flock and his mother's best friends. Maurice cringed as he recalled the pain and humiliation his mother suffered and the inadequacies he felt at not being able to protect her.

Images of his life began scrolling across his memory as if he was watching a movie. His earliest memory involved sitting on a church pew, playing quietly with a G.I. Joe action figure as his father expounded the word of God. The church would be crowded and hot with women waving white handkerchiefs. Though most of the parish would scream and yell while his father was preaching, Maurice's mother would sit quietly with her hands folded, occasionally nod her head and say a quiet "Amen". After services, Mrs. English would stand reverently by her husband at the exit door as the church members filed out. Maurice often wondered why most of the women ignored his mother, but always pumped his father's hand or hugged him or told him what a "blessing" his message had been. Inevitably, during Sunday dinners, one or another sister from the church would call, needing counseling on an urgent matter from the reverend. Maurice's father would always smile broadly, say he would be right there while his mother would develop a scowl on her face and stiffen her back. As the boys got older, Maurice noted how his eldest brother would begin mumbling under his breath on these occasions and some of his other brothers would make sarcastic remarks. His mother would shush them and go on about her afternoon chores. Afterwards though, Maurice would often hear soft cries coming from her bedroom and on occasion, had noted through the cracked door, her wringing her hands while tears coursed down her cheeks.

Reverend English felt bile in his throat as he reviewed his failure to make the choice to rescue his mom; to reveal his father for whom he really was and to ever truly rid himself of the hatred he often felt for his father. Yet, was he any better than his father??? Here he was feeling the strong pull of desire to respond to an emotional lover via his computer. No!!! He would not be his father. He would honor God, love his wife and be the minister he presented himself to the world to be. Reverend Maurice English looked at the computer screen, listened to the beckoning beep and with tears flowing down his cheeks, gently pushed the delete button.

Just as the reverend was pushing the delete button and feeling the relief and cleanliness of forgiveness, his wife, Mrs. Sarah English, was staring in shock at his office computer screen.

(Sarah & Maurice)

Sarah and Maurice met in their senior year of high school. She was immediately drawn to the good-looking, six foot four, silent, intelligent Maurice English. His soft, but commanding voice caused her heart to swell with anticipation and interest. When she learned he was one of the sons of the well-known and well-liked Reverend Maurice English, Sr., this only added to her excitement. She felt a prayer had been answered when he showed a mutual interest in her and asked her out on a date. Sarah and Maurice both had privileged lives; both were serious minded; both loved God and both had focused directions for their lives. As they became seriously involved, they discussed a marital future together to begin after earning their bachelor degrees from their respective colleges. He attended Morehouse in Atlanta and she attended Speilman. Maurice not only received his bachelor's, but eventually his master's in Theology. Sarah had majored in and received a bachelor's in business. Everything seemed to be going as planned until Maurice came to her, tearful and shaking as he shared what his home life was really like in reality. Sarah was shaken, yet felt compassion and hopeful as Maurice solemnly promised to "never" treat her as his father had treated his mother.

The Reverend and Mrs. English had had a blessed and fruitful life since then. They had six wonderful, successful children. In fact, their youngest child, a daughter, was in her final year of college. Sarah was looking forward to a time with 'just Maurice' again. She loved him being a minister and she loved that his congregation respected and sought him out, but now at last, he and she would be able to have some private couple time. Sarah was happily thinking of all of this as she and a sister from the church were cleaning and straightening her husband's church office. That's when she heard it—the soft beep of the computer indicating a message. Since the message was duplicated and would go directly to their home computer, she initially ignored it. Suddenly, however, she felt a strong urge to read this message. Trying to resist what she considered invasion of privacy and confidentiality, Sarah kept chatting with her friend, but the urge became stronger and stronger. Finally, she looked. She could not believe her eyes nor bear the sharp knife like feeling in her chest. As Sarah's knees buckled under, she dropped in a chair, believing she would never breathe or move again. There, before her very eyes, was one of the most explicit, intimate and sexual messages she had ever read—and it was written to her husband. The words "Yes, I, too, cannot wait to physically express my love to you" burned in her brain right before the screen suddenly went black.

From behind Mrs. English, she heard a quiet, but audible gasp. Her friend and church sister, whom she had forgotten was there, had seen the message, too. Sarah fretted over what she (her church sister) would now think of she and Reverend English, but her personal torment was so great, she did not think through on how to respond to her friend's knowledge of the situation.

When Sarah finally pulled herself together to go home, she realized she would have to confront her beloved Maurice. She knew all about his father and what she feared the most was now upon her—that Maurice would be like his father. As she drove home, her indescribable pain turned into a blind rage. How dare Maurice treat her this way; how dare he expound the word of God on Sundays, knowing what kind of things he had hidden in his heart. She felt anger that he had expressed what she had viewed as 'righteous indignation' towards his father when he was just like him. The only difference, as far as Sarah was concerned, was her father in law had not had the privilege of living in the age of computers.

By the time Sarah arrived home, she had gone through a rampant of emotions from being stunned to being devastated and embarrassed to feeling a pain like no other she had ever felt to being extremely angry to her present state: numbness. As she entered the home, Maurice was leaving his study. Her rage boiled over, for she knew exactly what he had been doing. Without forethought, Sarah ran towards Maurice and began pummeling him with her little fists. It did not hurt, but it did hold an element of surprise for Maurice and thus, knocked him off of his feet. When he fell, Sarah stood stock-still and with a look, which could only be described as livid, demanded to know what Maurice wanted to do about their marriage. Maurice was at a disadvantage since Sarah had entered the house and began attacking him physically emotionally without warning.

Maurice managed to catch his breath, get on his feet and sputter, "what are talking about, Sarah". The array of emotions for which Sarah had gone though in the past two hours, now left her spent. Her thought processes were activated and she became aware she had not even spoken to Maurice. She asked him to sit and said they needed to talk. Maurice sat gingerly in his recliner and mentally blocked himself from further attack. He himself was still trying to recover from the emotional turmoil of memories and having gained the strength to delete the unread message. He had no idea this was the very issue, which had prompted Sarah's attack on him.

Sarah began by inquiring if Maurice's feelings for her had changed; he said "no". She inquired if he was turning his back on God and he again said, "no". He then asked what this was all about. Instead of responding, Sarah asked if Maurice had used the computer that day. This resulted his hem hawing because technically, he did not use the computer—he looked at the screen and deleted the message unread. He, however, felt sick to the pit of his stomach and knew within his heart of hearts, that this unexpected rage from Sarah had something to do with the messages. Maurice evaded by inquiring what she meant. Sarah, stoically, repeated her question. Maurice said it was on, but he had not actually sat down at it and done any work. She suggested he might want to read his messages. With sinking heart, Maurice knew she knew, but he did not know how or how much. He asked Sarah why she said this; then with a flood of tears and sinking deep in her chair, Sarah hiccupped and told Maurice she had seen a duplicate message to him that included messages he had sent to the unknown woman, on his church computer. Maurice sobbed, begged for forgiveness and then inquired if Sarah would give him a chance to explain.

Maurice then confessed he had been talking with women via the computer for over a year. He said this was the only place he did not feel heavy responsibilities on his shoulder—it was an outlet. When on the computer, he felt like a young man with no identity, no responsibility, and no concerns. All of his contact had, thus, far, been only via email and were pure fantasy. He had felt no one was hurt this way, but in the past few weeks, he had begun feeling guilt and remorse. This was compounded when this last lady, decided she wanted a 'real relationship' with him. She was desirous of meeting him and had already suggested he needed a divorce. Maurice had actually been tempted to meet her and had made tentative plans. He knew she had sent him a message today, but he said he had been living his own childhood in his mind; had thought of his love and commitment to Sarah; become recognizant of the fact that this was spiritually, emotionally and morally wrong. That is why he had deleted the message without reading it. He suggested God had prevented him from deleting it before Sarah saw a copy for he knew he needed to confess to her and ask her forgiveness.

Sarah had much difficulty over the next few weeks, forgiving Maurice. She was suspicious of all of his phone calls and counseling sessions. The couple had to adjust and have Sarah check and respond to all phone and computer messages. Maurice had to report in a like a child. He felt resentful, but knew he had brought this upon himself. Interestingly enough as he began letting go of the resentment, Sarah seemed to begin softening up. The couple began praying together again and Maurice even confessed to the church that he had sinned against his profession and God and asked them for a public forgiveness. As time passed, Sarah began to feel forgiveness towards Maurice and began questioning him less and less. It would be years before she could forget what he had done, but she no longer felt suspicious about his every move or read more into everything he said than what he meant. With God's help, their marriage healed, but gone were the days of carefree love, trust and contentment. The nature of the relationship changed, but love and forgiveness allowed it to last them throughout their mortal lives. Temptations came, but were overcome and Reverend English became even more powerful in his ministry. What he did not know and would have been extremely distraught if he had, was this had a lasting impact on a young man in his congregation-a young man who only heard rumors and never understood the inner workings of an adult who was trying to please God, but had to work with his own past and his flesh nature.

(David)

That night all was quiet in the O'Brien home. Though David had been thinking about Reverend English's message and considering a change in his life, he still decided to 'sneak' out of the house. As he was passing his parents' bedroom, he could hear voices. He tiptoed to their room, pressed his ear against the door and then stifled the disappointed sob attempting to escape him as he learned of the flaw in Reverend English. According to his mother, God's right hand man had been having affairs. "No, no, no, not Reverend English!" reverberated in his mind. He could not believe his idol was a "mere mortal". David lost all desire to change and immediately ran out the door.

The weather was a match for David's tumultuous emotions. Outside it was stormy and inside of David, it was very stormy. David's clothes and hair were plastered to him. He, however, did not even notice because he was so distressed inwardly. Having already lost the innocence of childhood, David was looking for a "pick me upper". After wandering around for an indeterminate amount of time, David was unsuccessful in his search. This totally irritated and frustrated him. Life was the "pits"; it was not fair that kids did not have their own money to get what they needed/desired. Begrudgingly, David eventually gave up and headed for home.

Sneaking into the side door of the garage at his home, David noticed the old, abandoned refrigerator. This triggered his memory that his father sometimes would store his alcohol there in the "name of keeping it from the children"—he & Nelson, that is. Maybe, just maybe.... David quietly tiptoed to the refrigerator, slowly pulled open the creaking door and "bingo"!! He had definitely scored. He grabbed the bottle of rum and headed for the door leading into the house. David slipped into the side door, slid across the freshly shined kitchen floor and safely arrived in the hallway. He knew it would be smooth sailing from here to his room because the carpet there was so thick it would muffle his footsteps. Once in his room, David drained the whole bottle of rum or at least what was left of it. He then literally passed out in bed.

The next morning, David awakened to the chirping of birds. The sound felt as if it was splitting his head wide open. Sliding onto the floor out of bed, David moved urgently and as swiftly as possible to his bathroom. He then hid the bottle, dressed and headed outside for some fresh air.

Despite bis sometimes mature thinking/behavior, David was still a child. After his night of disappointments walking in the rain and forbidden imbibing of alcohol, David was feeling extremely distraught and physically ill. He had vomited, washed his face, taken 'baby aspirin' and drank juice that looked like tomato juice as he had seen his father do, but his ten year old body could not handle the liquor he had consumed—he was hung over!

Knowing he could not let his mother see him, David waited until he heard her in the shower. He, then, shouted through the door to her, that he was going out to play with Nelson. Even his own voice caused his head to pound and swim, but he was still able to get out the door, though stumbling over his own feet.

Little David had engaged in adult behavior and was attempting to numb this unidentifiable pain in an adult manner, but he was a child. His mind buzzing, his stomach sick and his thinking eschewed, David went looking for Nelson. A few blocks before getting to Nelson's neighborhood, David heard a commotion. He looked towards the noise near the abandoned ball field and saw several big boys circling something or someone. As he edged closer, he heard taunts of "Hey retardo, what you gonna do? You gonna call your mommy? Waa waa waa! Little four eyed retardo needs mommy to blow his nose and hold his hand". Through his befuddled thinking and slight blurred vision, David saw these guys were picking on Nelson. Without thinking, he barreled at them with his body while holding his trusted pocketknife in his hand. He was so unstable on his feet, he could not have done anything, but it was to his advantage that he took the guys off guard. They heard this banshee-like screaming coming at them, as well as saw the glint of a knife, not knowing it was nothing more than a dull pocket knife. They scattered and left Nelson alone.

Nelson stood stunned for a brief moment, not knowing from where his salvation had come. Suddenly, he saw his idol, his best friend. "Davie", Nelson screamed. "Thank you, Davie, thank you. Nelson love Davie. Nelson do something for Davie." David asked Nelson if he would do anything he asked to prove his loyalty. Nelson looked closer at David and saw he looked funny, but he still said yes. David, still feeling upset and slightly intoxicated decided Nelson should prove his loyalty. About that time, a stray, straggly looking cat walked down the sidewalk. This looked like that same cat that was always coming into their yard. David's mom often commented on how she wished that cat would stay away from the house. She knew it was homeless and feared it might be carrying some diseases. Fury and rage still simmering about the minister, as well as the influence of alcohol on his little body caused David to make a rash, mean decision.

"Nelson really want to help Davie?" he asked. Nelson nodded cheerfully and vigorously. "Kill that cat". Nelson's eyes widened and fear shook his body. There was really something wrong with Davie, but he kept insisting he kill the cat. Nelson chased the cat, caught him and slowly picked him up. He began rubbing his scraggly fur and with large tears rolling down his face, pleaded with

David, "Nelson not hurt the kitty, Nelson not hurt the kitty". David, however, would not back down, telling Nelson he saved his butt and if Nelson really loved him, he'd do it. Quickly and as gently as he could, Nelson snapped the cat's neck and let it slide to the ground. David, suddenly sobering up, realized what he had done both to the cat and to Nelson. Doubling over from both physical and emotional distress, David vomited all over the ground. He felt so bad, but did not know how to correct it. In an effort to at least make it up to Nelson, he grabbed Nelson's hand, pulled him down the road with him and offered to buy him some ice-cream.

Nelson, now sobbing almost inconsolably, went with David, but felt some fear. He had never seen David like this; he had never hurt anything before and had never believed David would either. As they arrived at the ice-cream parlor, David gathered his pride together, apologized to Nelson and the two boys began punching each other as boys will do when emotionally overwhelmed. Neither ever forgot this day, though they never spoke of it again either. This incident actually prevented them from ever doing anything of this nature again.

CHAPTER SIX

The Teacher

After being so devastated over the summer by the trauma of learning how his idol, Reverend English, was not perfect, David withdrew more than ever into himself. He was developing a hard shell of self-protection. David had made up his mind no one would get next to him or make him do anything he did not want to do. School was hard for him, but he no longer cared—he was not going to try to do his work. David had plans to become invisible again during fifth grade. He once thought he wanted to be noticed, but he now knew he did not.

Staring stony faced and stiff-necked from his little desk, David reluctantly felt the stoniness dissipating when he met Mr. Rochester. Mr. Rochester, a suave, slim, brown skinned African American, not unlike David himself, had gentle eyes and a compassionate demeanor. David watched and listened guardedly for weeks, but found himself being drawn more and more to Mr. Rochester. His schoolwork improved because he wanted to impress and please Mr. Rochester. For the first time David thought about a future. He wanted to emulate Mr. Jayson Rochester and become a teacher like him.

Mr. Rochester was, also, like a surrogate father to David. He seemed to have more time for him and showed an interest in his schoolwork. What David was too young to understand was his parents loved him and wanted him to do well in school—they just were so caught up in trying to make a living for the family, they had no time. In addition, his parents had never had the opportunity to further their own educations after completing high school.

Crouching over his desk, David was concentrating on his English test and furiously writing out his responses. He wanted Mr. Rochester to be proud of him. He wanted his answers to be neat, well thought out and correct. His parents did not encourage him in his schoolwork, but Mr. Rochester did and told him he could be somebody. As these thoughts raced through his mind, he felt the familiar and comforting pressure of Mr. Rochester' hand on his shoulder. He often did this with his students so they would know he was there, available and ready to help should they run into problems with their work or actually with any problem at all.

Mr. Jayson Rochester had been voted "Teacher of the Year" twice in his professional career. He would never have imagined something like this happening to him when he was growing up; though on the surface, his life looked good. He, however, was tormented by his childhood demons. He felt as if he was always "looking over his shoulder". He inwardly lived his life waiting for the "bomb to drop".

Jayson was the middle child of three in the Rochester family. His siblings were both girls and Jayson often felt responsible for them. To this day, he would mentally beat himself up for what he perceived as his failure to "protect them". Jayson also never learned appropriate love between males—no knowledge of father/son relationship.

Mr. and Mrs. Rochester were not exactly "parents of the year". Jayson recalled many nights when he would grab his sisters and they would all crouch in the closet while waiting for the fighting to stop. Th would all try to be very, very quiet for if they were not, dad would then start in on them. He mainly pulled, hit and yelled at the girls. As for Jayson, he usually acted as if he did not even exist. Jayson sometimes wished his dad would hit him just for the physical contact and attention.

Jayson's dad worked maintenance positions all of Jayson's life. His mother often performed menial tasks, as ironing and baking for others as an additional source of income. In reality, the couple made enough money to support the basic needs of their family of five, but they mismanaged the money. This resulted in numerous fights, which in turn, resulted in Jayson's mom drinking more. When his mom would drink herself into a coma, if his dad was still upset, this is when the abuse of the girls would begin. Overall, Jayson's father was the stereotyped abuser and his mother the textbook alcoholic.

By the time Jayson was thirteen, he had begun coping with the lack of paternal love and maternal protection, by immersing himself in his schoolwork. He, also, chose to assist with the younger Boy Scout organizations. Jayson thought this might be a way to make up for lack of protection for his sisters. He was very awkward with girls and had fleeting insight that this was probably due to lack of role modeling from his parents.

At age fourteen, Jayson's mom died while he and his sisters were at school. Death was ruled accidental. She fell down the stairs in their creaky, run down townhouse and broke her neck. There were signs of alcohol in her system. Jayson, however, was never sure if she fell down drunk or if his father pushed her. His father had been in the home when this occurred and the only statement he ever made was "she fell, stupid drunk". Jayson felt so many conflicting emotions: he was happy for his mom to not have to put up with his father anymore; he was angry she never protected him and now was gone and he was guilty for not feeling only sadness.

As difficult as it was to imagine or believe, life actually became more horrendous in the Rochester household after his mother's death. Though the alcoholic dramas ceased, the abuse did not. In fact, it took on a new nature. Now, not only did Jayson's dad yell at and hit Jayson's sisters, he now turned inappropriate affection on them. Jayson's eldest sister, who was now sixteen became more aggressively violent towards Jayson. This violence was mainly verbal, but it really cut him to the heart because he wanted to protect her so much. Jayson believed his sister was angry with him for failure to protect her when they were younger. In later years, he learned she was acting out her anger, humiliation and frustration against the one person who would not hurt her. It was years before he could see or understand this. He, thus, felt as if he was the ultimate failure. His only source of comfort came from Scout Masters and being allowed to assist with the younger kids in the tiger scouts. The tiger scouts came before the cub scouts and the little boys in their orange and blue uniforms were so trusting, innocent and admiring, Jayson felt himself drawn more and more to them.

As fourteen turned to fifteen and fifteen to sixteen, Jayson found himself thinking he should get involved with females, but still too shy and nervous; plus, in reality, he had no interest in dating them. Life experiences had taught him females needed protection and he was not able to do this. He had never seen his father be affectionate and loving towards his mother so he did not have the least idea on how to approach a woman. Though he was not sure what the emotions were that surfaced when he was around males, especially the younger ones, he just knew with males, he felt warm, secure and lovable.

Jayson completed high school without one stable relationship or flirtation. He had tried to date a couple of girls and though they responded favorably, he found himself uninterested time and time again. Females often approached Jayson because he was so gentle and he was very attractive. He felt bad when he could not give them what they wanted. Again, as with his sisters and mom, he was failing the female species. His male friends boasted of their conquests and tried to get Jayson to share his. Jayson would shrug and say a "gentleman never kisses and tells", but in reality, he had nothing to share. He, in fact, was much more interested in his male comrades. Not only did he find them more interesting; moreover he lost the feeling of the need to "protect". With his male buddies, he was just Jayson. Jayson, whom they thought, was probably "scoring with the ladies", but maybe really did have too much class to talk. These guys, in reality, despite the bantering and teasing, really admired him for this stand. Repetitively, Jayson's only validation of admiration and success came from the male sector. He did not intentionally focus on this fact; however, it was always in his subconscious.

Jayson graduated from high school with honors; not that it mattered to anyone in his family. His eldest sister never came home anymore and his younger sister was sinking further and further into the depths of alcoholism. His father plain and simply, did not care as long as he had food to eat, women to chase and did not have to engage in parental behaviors. The night of graduation, therefore, was also Jayson's last night at home. He hated to forsake his sisters, but he could not protect or help them anyway. He had one aspiration—to get away! Jayson had been accepted to a nearby university; had received grants and scholarships to major in elementary education and had obtained a summer job on campus to begin at once. Jayson boarded a bus instead of attending the high school graduation party. His father actually did not miss him for days and then only because he noticed the house being in disarray. He, nevertheless, never sought out Jayson and Jayson only made menial attempts to keep contact with his sisters.

College was wonderful for Jayson. There were diversities of race, sexual orientation, economics, etc. He finally felt he was at home. This attitude made him popular with both faculty and co-eds alike. He excelled in his studies and was overjoyed when he did his student teaching at a private school for boys. Throughout his college years, Jayson never felt the stirrings for females and still experienced the warm fuzzies for certain male co-harts and for the "little boys" with whom he came in contact. Jayson had no intentions of acting on these emotions, but neither did he berate himself in private anymore for having them.

After obtaining his undergraduate degree in Elementary Education, Jayson enrolled in some graduate classes while seeking employment. With the g.p.a. Jayson maintained, the shortage of males in this field and his attitude, he had no problem attaining employment. Best of all, he got his first choice of fifth grade.

Jayson threw himself into his graduate studies and his teaching. This left no room for the pain of family isolation or the sense of failure he had lived with most of his life. Within two years of teaching, he was nominated Teacher of the Year. What no one knew was the warm fuzzy heat of being with the little boys was surfacing in full force. Jayson had no desire to hurt anyone so had no intentions of breaking his vow not act on this; it, however, was becoming more and more tempting to simply stroke their hair, rub their little hands and squeeze their thighs. It was so rewarding to see the smiles and admiration in their eyes in response to his rubbing, squeezing and fondling. Jayson found himself having dreams about the various children and they were all romantic or sexual in nature. Upon awakening, he would think this was not acceptable, but when drifting to sleep at night, the pictures and thoughts would vividly return.

As each school year melted into the next, Jayson found himself more and more intrigued by the various little ones. He was most drawn to the ones who seemed to be unhappy or who had problems with their studies. He would make a special effort with these children and was always rewarded with hugs, smiles and I love you. He had been spending much time with David O'Brien and received such a powerful response of loyalty and adoration from this cute, brown eyed lost soul, he did not know if he could control himself. Jayson, however, had always made it a practice to never let the temptation draw him further into the forbidden realms with children in his classroom. Where he failed, was with children on the playground.

His fifth graders, along with another class of fifth graders and two classes of fourth graders, had recess together. Mr. Rochester, being so popular, always had the shy, lonely children circling him and wrapping their arms around his midriff. This is where much of the more intense fondling, rubbing and squeezing would take place; yet still with some decorum because other teachers were within his view. One day, after school, however, it suddenly dawned on Jayson how many of the little boys were left after school for thirty to forty minutes waiting on their rides home. He began offering the parents his supervision of these children or even to drop them off at home. Most were so relieved by the offer of help, they agreed. This is when he crossed the line.

All of the children had left the school late one Friday afternoon, with the exception of the green eyed, reddish brown haired, petite little boy standing off to the side. Mr. Rochester inquired if he had a ride home and he burst into tears. He was not sure if his mom had forgotten him and he was scared. Mr. Rochester took him into the school, located his registration card and called the cell phone number listed for his mom. She was so relieved when he called because she was in traffic and there was not an answer when she would attempt to call the school. Mr. Rochester volunteered his help and it was accepted. When he told the child he would take him home, the tears abated and he threw his arms around Mr. Rochester and said "I wuv you". This child was only in the second grade and he made Mr. Rochester feel so awesome.

Jayson's memory of that day was now muddled with cloudiness, self-deprecation and humiliation. As he and the child headed for his home, the child moved closer to Mr. Rochester and leaned against his shoulder. When they arrived at the large, stately home, Jayson wondered why this child seemed so deprived and lonely. It soon became apparent for this second grader had his own key and no one was home, (the daily routine was for mom to pick him up at school; drop him off at home and then she or his dad would be home an hour or so later) He asked if Mr. Rochester could stay awhile. He proudly showed off his house and room—he was an only child and had all of the material things he could want. He asked Mr. Rochester if he wanted cookies and milk and they had a snack. As they watched afternoon cartoons, the little boy snuggled next to the teacher. Without rational thought,

Jayson began tousling the little boy's hair, snuggling next to him and began fondling his privates. The little boy felt uncomfortable, but this was Rochester, so he did not say anything Jayson was so wrapped up in the ecstasy, he did not notice the fear or hesitancy. The only thing that snapped him out of his reverie was the sound of a car pulling up. He pulled himself together, hugged the little boy to his chest and then went to meet the child's mom. She fell all over herself expressing gratitude and Jayson left.

Over the weekend, the child's mom noticed he seemed more withdrawn and when she would mention Mr. Rochester, he would tense up, tear up or simply go to his room. Though on the surface, it may have seemed she did not care for her child, she loved him very much and was sensitive to his needs and moods. Eventually, she mentioned the child's reaction to her husband and her husband gently approached him by reading a child's book about a little boy who was touched inappropriately by an uncle. The child began hiccupping and crying and finally confessed to what had happened. After reassuring him he had done nothing wrong and they loved him, the parents contacted the school board and the principal. It took a whole week before they finally approached Mr. Rochester, but the time did arrive.

(David)

The day was almost over and David felt good about his work. He believed he aced his English test. Towards the end of the day while listening to Mr. Rochester during story time, he could barely wait for the bell to ring so he could talk to Mr. Rochester privately. About that time, though, the principal called Mr. Rochester out into the hall. There were men in suits out there, as well as a young boy who appeared to be hiding behind his mother's skirts. Then David saw someone who struck fear in his heart—it was a man in the standard blue uniform of policemen. Why were they talking to Mr. Rochester? What did they want with him? "Leave him alone, just leave him alone", David thought in his mind. The group walked off and Mrs. Smith from next door came into their classroom. No one told the classroom of children anything—she simply dismissed them when the bell rang.

David ran home with the sweat of running down his arms and legs. What had happened? How could he find out? He did not have to wait long, for on the six o'clock news, he heard the most unbelievable, most horrific thing!!! "It was not true, it had to be a lie!!! It just had to be, didn't it????" The news anchor was spreading the vicious rumor that Mr. Rochester was a child molester. With this news and staring at the leading news story of Mr. Rochester, David felt his heart began to harden again and he slowly began building an emotional wall of bricks around himself.

From that point, David showed little interest in school. The classroom got a new teacher for the rest of the school year. Their new school teacher was a vivacious, pretty, young woman, but David did not care. All of the other students flocked around her and soon forgot Mr. Rochester, but not David. He forever held the image of the news story in his head and heart. Whenever he would find himself trusting an adult, he would quickly pull this memory out so as to protect himself.

CHAPTER SEVEN

The Neighbors

David had begun engaging in more dangerous delinquent behaviors. He had moved from just playing pranks and stealing from the local grocer, to actually pick pocketing and attempting to break into homes. Recently a couple of females had moved in next door to David. David did not know their names and did not care. He had watched them moving so as to scope out what possessions of interest they may have had. Since they were females, he was not sure if they would have anything interesting, such as stereo equipment or other items he could pawn. He, however, watched their daily activities and began making tentative plans within his head to take what he could, whenever the opportunity presented itself. And the opportunity would present itself; he knew patience and watchfulness always paid off for him.

Twelve-year old David patiently watched as the neighbors left their home. He waited until he felt it was safe before attempting to break into their home. While waiting, he engaged in curious thoughts concerning the 'lesbian-like' couple, but soon dismissed this thought process so as to gain unnoticed entry into their home. What he was too young to observe and/or understand, this couple had suffered much pain and was simply attempting to regain a sense of life for themselves.

(Marsha & Krista)

The resounding sound of the slap across her face was the straw that broke the camel's back. Marsha thought if she had to feel that sting one more time or endure the guilt rendering words spewing from her mother's mouth, she would go into a murderous rage. At age forty-one, it was time for her to "leave the nest". She had already missed a lifetime of opportunities for marriage, children, career, etc… The perfect opportunity for escape had knocked on her door—a group mission for God. Working for God had to be a better alternative than resorting to murder.

With steely determination riding her spine and written on her face, Marsha spoke in a deceptively sweet voice as she told her mother that she no longer had the power over her. Marsha, then, picked up her shabby bag and walked out the door to never return as an inhabitant to that home again.

Arriving at the bus depot, Marsha noticed the cherub faced young lady, also boarding the bus. She seemed so carefree and happy, Marsha was immediately drawn to her. Looking closer, however, Marsha realized there was some sadness peering from behind those dark soulful eyes. She still, nevertheless, gravitated towards this young woman.

As Marsha and Krista sat side by side on the bus, neither understood they were two strangers embarking on a common journey—a journey to help others, while escaping and healing from their own private, painful pasts. Neither was aware of how comfortably intertwined their lives would soon be.

The other bus passengers noticed the two youngish appearing women. Their impression was these were two young women who must have hearts of gold to sacrifice their time in order to do "religious duties" and "help others". What the casual observer could not see nor know was these battered hearts of gold had dents scratches, rust spots and chinks.

Marsha and Krista hit it off so well, it was hard to believe they had just met each other. Both indicated it seemed as if they had known each other in a previous life. They would often feel they were experiencing de ja vu over the next few years. By the time the bus arrived in Middle Tennessee from the Western U.S., Krista and Marsha had decided they would try to find an apartment together to cut down on the expenses and to not feel so alone and alienated in a foreign land.

Over the next few months, the two continued to get along, but were beginning to discover differences between them. The most apparent one, yet the one overlooked the most was their chosen style of dress. Not only did their attires expose their personalities, but the chosen styles were also representative of their upbringings. Marsha, who was raised to always put her best foot forward, tended to dress more formal. She found it unbearable to be seen without having properly showered, dressed for the public and be outwardly put together. Krista, on the other hand was much more laid back, feeling her most comfortable in sweats and tennis shoes. Krista bad grown up on a farm where it was unreasonable to be dressed in hose, pumps and dresses. Though this would appear to not be significant, it was, because it simply reflected more of who each of these persons were.

Krista tended to be lighthearted on the surface and it appeared nothing bothered or effected her. Marsha, on the other hand, just as represented by her style of dress, was more serious and seemed to be affected deeper by her environment. Interestingly enough, each later learned both was probably as affected by environment and inner turmoil, but they simply responded in a different manner.

Growing up, Marsha had always had to be perfect. She had taken on responsibilities well beyond what she should have done. By age seven, Marsha actually was taking care of her mother. Her mother was not an invalid, but she had been in an abusive and unhappy relationship with Marsha's dad. In Marsha's young mind, she connected her father's behavior to her own and believed this was why mom was so unhappy. She, thus, would do everything in her power, to be mom's support system. Role reversal of parent/child took place much earlier than it should have. When Marsha's dad finally left the home by the time Marsha was nine, she was wise beyond her years. By then, she knew her dad had girlfriends, was not supporting the family and if her mom would confront him, he would hit her to shut her up". Marsha still felt some guilt about this, though why she was blaming herself, she did not know why—she just believed somehow she could have and should have changed the situation. Marsha felt guilty, also, because when her dad left, she was actually glad. This gladness caused her to withdraw so people could not discover her deep dark secret of happiness. It, also, resulted in her overcompensating by spending more time taking care of mom and trying to insure her (mom's) happiness.

Though on the surface, Krista's childhood appeared much more normal than Marsha's, it was not. It was actually as devastating, but in a different way. Krista had always acted like a happy go lucky person, smiling at everyone while keeping herself occupied. She engaged in solitary activities on the farm and preferred the company of the animals and the outdoors to being with groups of children and family.

Krista was not shy; she was of the melancholic nature that allowed her to be contented with herself. Due to this, she would frequent the barn where she would read, write, draw and talk with the stable animals. Her happiness shone through her eyes and her behavior so people were attracted to her. By age ten, the cherub faced, Gerber looking child would skip through the yard unaffected by her environment or how she herself looked. All this did was attract more people to her, especially males. Men would see this cheerful, cute little girl who did not mind getting dirty and want to be around her. Most men recognized this as pleasure at the innocence of children. One farmhand, however, had a darker side and viewed it more sexual. He knew Krista spent hours in the barn amongst the haystacks and he knew her parents did not stress; after all, they lived in a very small, safe community where everyone knew everyone. Late, one afternoon, Grayson sauntered into the barn and casually inquired of Krista what she was doing. Without looking up, she responded cheerfully that she was reading a book on horses. Krista had a dream that one day she would own and breed horses. Grayson asked if he could join her and she motioned for him to sit as she continued to be immersed in her book. Suddenly, she felt strange hands on her neck, rubbing her. She glanced around and moved slightly away. She did not know what was wrong with Grayson, but she decided to ignore it. When Krista moved, nonetheless, Grayson moved with her. Finally, Krista, in her straightforward way, told him to stop; she was busy and she did not like to be touched. Inside, Krista felt jittery and nauseated. She was too young to know why, but she knew this was not right. This did not feel the same as when the older guys would swing her around or horseplay with her or even hoist her onto the horses. Looking around the darkening barn, Krista realized dusk had arrived. She, also, realized she had moved into a position where Grayson was between her and the exit. Panic set in her throat and chest and she began wheezing. Grayson backed away and Krista ran into the house. When her mom saw her and asked what was wrong, she told her, her stomach hurt and she needed to lie down. Krista could barely sleep all night, tossing and turning and wondering what it all meant.

At age ten, Krista was beginning to understand everything was not necessarily right with the world. By this same time, Marsha was fourteen and truly understood this. She knew life was not fair. She had lost her childhood, taking care of her mom and trying to protect her from her father. Now at fourteen, instead of spending giggly times with her girlfriends talking about boys, Marsha had made it her mission to find someone for her mother. Maybe, she could find a man who would love her mother, take care of her and then Marsha could be a teenager. If she found the right guy this time, she would not run him off or make him be mean to her mom like she somehow did with her biological father. Marsha actually had an older brother and a younger sister, but being the middle child, she also acted as the peacemaker. Her siblings went on with their lives and as is typical of most children, did not feel concern about anything that did not directly affect them.

As time passed, Krista and Marsha learned more and more about each other's private pains. Some of this resulted as trust between the two developed and allowed them to open up. Other times, pasts surfaced due to them running into similar incidents that would trigger their own childhood memories.

Much of Marsha and Krista's ministry dealt with teens and children. They usually were very helpful to these young souls because of their own unique upbringings. One day, Marsha was shaken to her core for memories she thought she had longed suppressed raced to the surface of her consciousness like a runaway train. Marsha and Krista had been assigned to a family with three teenagers. The middle child was a young girl about seventeen years old. When they entered the home, the mom was lying on the sofa, barking orders. The eldest girl and younger boy were simply continuing to do what they wanted. The middle child, to whom Marsha was drawn, was the only one responding to mom.

Angel, as the girl was called, looked so worn and tired to only be seventeen. Marsha felt the tugging at her heart and the recesses of her mind. She had been Angel once. She had been the one who had to respond to all of mom's beckoning for her siblings would live their lives regardless of what mom said. Marsha was the only one who felt guilt and responsibility. Seeing Angel look and respond the way Marsha had, she was catapulted back to when she was seventeen.

Marsha was entering her senior year of High school. She felt as if she had missed out on the best years of her life. Marsha had not joined social clubs or cliques. She had no best friend and she had not attended any of the high school functions. This was not because she did not want to, but because she felt obligated to spend all of her spare time, attending to mom. Her siblings had done all of the adolescent things, but not Marsha. She spent her high school years, cleaning, cooking, comforting mom and trying to find a mate for mom. Every since her dad had gone, Marsha had tried in vain repetitively to "replace him" with someone nice and lovable. Instead of her dating guys, she was trying to find guys for her mom to date. Marsha would check out older men at the library when studying, the grocery store when shopping for the family and department stores when purchasing clothing for the family. She worked at a ticket booth at the local movie theatre and she would always look at the ring fingers of the older gentlemen who would come to the movies alone. Surprisingly enough, though she would not approach anyone for herself, she never hesitated to approach guys for her mom. She was desperate to make mom happy so she could have her own life. Marsha had actually succeeded in setting her mom up on several dates, but always, mom would find something wrong with them after two or three dates. She began to feel it was hopeless and she herself would never have a life.

It was the year she was seventeen that Marsha found herself wanting desperately to date. She had noticed a transfer student in her English class. He seemed so sophisticated and debonair. He, also, was not from her hometown so he had no preconceived ideas about her and her family. He did not know about her mom and how Marsha had betrayed her by running their dad away. Marsha felt a desire to "fix herself up" and to be attractive when she would see him. He would smile at and nod to her when he saw her in the hallways. Marsha found herself day-dreaming about him during class and when attempting to do her chores at home. When at the movie theatre, selling tickets, she would envision herself with him when couples would come to her window. She would watch the romance movies and in her mind, superimpose hers and his images on the screen as if the couple was the two of them. Marsha finally got up the nerve to tell her mother she had met someone. Her mother went ballistic, asking her if she had not learned anything from her own relationships. She told Marsha she did not want her to make the same mistakes she had. Guys were deceitful and only wanted one thing and Marsha knew what that was. She battered Marsha emotionally daily until Marsha lost all courage to even try to get to know her classmate. Marsha decided she would not ever have the opportunity to have a life as long as mom was alive. Apparently, her lot in life was to care for her mom in order to make up for having run her father away.

As Marsha looked at Angel she saw herself at seventeen and immediately wanted to "rescue" her. She decided she would intervene and not let Angel suffer the next twenty years of her life as Marsha had. She, in fact, was able to intervene and by the end of her mission with Angel's family, Marsha felt a sense of success and contentment. Not only did Angel listen to Marsha, she actually applied to, was accepted to college and stood up to her irate mom. This, in turn, actually resulted in Angel's mom developing some personal esteem and some pride in Angel once she got over her standing up to her.

Krista had noted and been very aware of Marsha's keen interest and dedication to Angel. When she finally inquired why she seemed so intense about her, Marsha had shared the flashback to when she herself had been seventeen. This caused Krista to think she could share more of her childhood trauma with Marsha. Until she met Marsha, she had tried to run from all of these distressing memories. She decided now was the time to start coping with her own private demons and she knew the way to do this was to talk about it.

Recently, Krista had been dreaming about the time in the barn with Grayson. Memories long suppressed were breaking their way through her subconscious into her nocturnal hours of sleep. She took a figurative cavernous breath and allowed the flooding of her mind to occur.

After fleeing the barn and having a restless night, Krista began to view the world differently. Overnight, she lost the innocence of childhood and learned of tumultuous emotions no ten-year old should know. Krista became withdrawn and though she continued to be interested in horses, she spent less time with them and spent more time simply drawing pictures of them from the safety of her room. Krista's parents, being the loving and aware parents they were, noted this disturbing change in Krista and attempted to find out what happened. Krista remained closemouthed and withdrawn. Her parents finally decided to just watch, be as aware as possible and fervently hope that this was just a preadolescent stage through which Krista was going.

As pre-teen years melted into teen years, Krista continued to remain quiet. It seemed she made a special effort to not appear female. She would wear lots of oversized clothing; refused make-up and almost seemed to abhor the male species. Her mom coaxed her to 'dress like a lady' to no avail. Her father was relieved that she had no interest in such; he felt this gave him one less worry-girls with too much interest in makeup, clothing and boys seemed to get too distracted from important things, like school, and too often, ended up pregnant. He, therefore, always took Krista's side when she would argue with mom about her chosen dress.

Despite the fighting against growing into a young lady, Krista's body still did and eventually her hormones surfaced. By age sixteen, Krista was no longer the poster child Gerber baby in appearance; rather she was tall, with long dark hair, tanned skin and dark haunting eyes. Ironically, she still maintained a modicum of the look of a cherub. This drew the teen boys to her as well as older men, not unlike Grayson, Krista dated almost nonstop; she, nevertheless, never gave her heart. She was always cautious and still very uncomfortable if a guy would hug her or try to kiss her. She actually became known as a tease. In reality, she was dealing with a kaleidoscope of emotions: having the hormones of a teenage girl, but the experience of when she was ten with Grayson and thus, fear of anything beyond harmless flirtation.

Krista's mom felt relief at her new interest in males and her dad felt the normal horror most dads of girls feel when their daughters reach this stage. He was his most relieved when she hit age nineteen and began dating a nice young man on a rather exclusive basis. He felt safer this way.

Krista dated Mark for six months before she ever let him kiss her. When he actually waited for her and did not pressure her, she let some of her guard down with him. She began to feel she could get over the trauma at ten and this was a guy she could trust. Besides, he was a year younger and this somehow, helped Krista feel a little more in control of the situation. The couple dated another twelve months and after much persuasion by Mark, Krista married him.

During the time Krista was being a newlywed and trying to be a housewife with normal feelings, Marsha was becoming more and more resigned to her life with mom. She had dated several guys when she was in her twenties, but mom always sabotaged the relationships. She would become ill when Marsha had a date or she would interrogate the young men to the degree they would not call Marsha back out of fear. Marsha watched one potential relationship after the other walk out the door, the reason always had something to do with mom. Marsha began operating in automation mode and giving up on having her own life. She thought she had resolved this in her mind and could live this way until the day she walked out to become part of the church mission.

While Marsha had resigned her life to being with mom, Krista was being the newlywed. She tried desperately to be a normal, happy housewife. She settled into cooking and cleaning and being the stereotyped housewife for the first few months. Though she felt a void in her life, it was not that difficult to do because she really cared for Mark. He was a fairly affable and easygoing person. He seemed to really adore Krista and he was never pushy. As time passed, nevertheless, Mark became more sexually aggressive and pushy. He, also, began to act "macho" and kept talking about how "he was the man of the house". Some of this seemed to be influenced by his male co-workers and some of it stemmed from his simply growing up.

As time passed, Krista became really frustrated with Mark's attitude, as well as "just being a housewife" and decided she was ready to begin working with horses again. When she broached this topic with Mark, he went completely ballistic. "No wife of mine is going to work" he stormed. "No normal woman would want to be sweaty and nasty smelling by working with horses. Besides that, working with horses, was man's work. It was time for Krista to have a baby. She needed a baby, not a horse". The couple would go round and round with this topic to no avail.

Krista's parents would note her distress and felt bad. Krista's mom tried to understand, but her parents were "old school" and did not fully understand why Krista was so opposed to being a wife and another. Her mom had to admit some of this may have been their fault since they raised her on a farm and never discouraged her from being a "tomboy". Her mom, however, really believed it was more to it than this. She had never forgotten the odd night when Krista was ten and would not talk with her. From that night on, Krista had seemed different—nothing one could put a finger on, but just different. She had withdrawn at that point and was never as outgoing as she used to be. Her mom had contributed it to "growing up", but maternal instinct had told her it was more. She wondered if maybe it was time to talk to her about this again.

Mark and Krista's marriage deteriorated. They went through the motions of being married, but both knew it was not going to work. Krista continued to refuse to become impregnated and would not give up her desire to work with horses. After two years of arguing over this, Krista simply went to work with horses without Mark's permission. She ignored everyone's advice and remained closemouthed about what had happened to her so many years ago. Mark became cold and withdrawn or he would verbally and emotionally attack Krista. Krista withdrew into her emotional shell and threw herself into her job working on the ranch doing horse grooming.

After a year of the marriage dying, Krista waited patiently to bury it, while Mark tried to aggressively keep it breathing. He did not really care about the marriage; it was his egotistical pride that kept him from allowing it to die a natural death. Finally, Mark met a woman who acted as if she adored him. She was feminine, rather dopey acting; kept talking about how she really wanted children and to "please her man". Mark thought if he flaunted Susannah in Krista's face, she would fight for him. Actually, Krista felt relief that he had turned his attention elsewhere; that way, she could fully devote her time and attention to her beloved horses. When Mark realized Krista was not changing, and Susannah was pressuring him to be a family, he "told" Krista he was divorcing her. He did not "ask", but "told" her because he thought this kept him in control. Krista, however, did not try to stop the divorce, happily signed the papers and moved into an efficiency apartment.

From that point on, Krista kept primarily to herself, worked on the horse ranch until male chauvinism got to her and she, like Marsha, eventually found herself boarding a bus for a church mission.

Krista and Marsha met up; shared their lives; were very effective in the mission and found themselves lifetime friends. Eventually, they were both able to resolve their individual issues and be of benefit to others. They had been through so much in their lives, so when they got home that afternoon and found their house had been broken into, they took it in stride.

Now after many years of seeking, helping and suffering, Krista and Marsha wore hearts that were not like new, but were like a patchwork quilt made with precious memories. The "odes" Marsha used to write were now pure "poetry". The need Krista used to have to "blunt her emotions" was now "an open book to be read". Were these two lesbians??? NO—but through each other they had learned what it means to give and receive pure love.

David was successful in entering the neighbor's home, stole a few items he thought he could sell and returned to his home. He never knew what life problems his neighbors had endured.

Though Krista and Marsha suspected David, they did not confront him nor his parents. They had observed David just as he had them. Both, intuitively, felt he was troubled and seeking attention. They often wondered if they were doing him any favors by not confronting him, but decided to forget the incident and let it ride.

David, feeling powerful and confident that he had once again "ruled" over someone and gotten away with it, continued his petty thievery. Eventually, he did get tired of it, but he continued for awhile.

As he was turning into an adolescent, however, David's interests began to include girls. He was not as interested in juvenile antics, now that he had a newfound interest—the female species.

CHAPTER EIGHT

The Girlfriend

Being held over in juvenile until court time had given David more time than he desired to experience regrets and worries. He continued to recall specific events and persons in his life. He, presently, was worried about his girlfriend. Would she still be his support system now that he would be away for awhile?? Would she visit with him and be waiting with open arms upon his release??? He desperately hoped so as he began recalling meeting her for the first time.

David and Nelson had gone to the arcade on that lazy Saturday afternoon. David was then thirteen and felt he was "a man". He had already experienced many adult things well beyond his chronological age, but as all must, he still had typical hormonal changes/growth to occur. The primary reason he and Nelson chose the arcade for this afternoon outing involved girls. Nelson absolutely loved the games. David enjoyed getting his aggressions out through the games, too, but he also knew there might be girls there to impress with his game prowess. As nature does, however, he was called by it soon after arriving. He told Nelson to "stay put"; he would be right back.

While David was in the restroom, Nelson decided to see if he could begin the games on his own. He, of course, had some troubles and was feeling frustrated when help arrived.

Just as Nelson was receiving help, David walked out to see this unbelievably beautiful goddess showing Nelson how to get the coins in the machine. David could not believe his eyes. This was the most gorgeous dark haired, olive skinned, shapely creature he had ever seen. When she turned her large dark, almond shaped eyes in his direction, he almost passed out with breathlessness. Everything seemed to be moving in slow motion and David felt himself mesmerized by this vision of loveliness. He, however, resorted to cockiness when approaching her in order to "not lose his cool". After mumbling some mundane question about her giving him her seven digits, he learned from Nelson that this goddess had a name—Daniella.

(Daniella & David)

The meeting of Daniella and David was very similar to the one of his mother and father. David and his dad were both taken off guard by their own overwhelming emotions at the sight of these females. Both had almost identical thoughts about these two females—using almost the exact words to describe them upon seeing them for the first time. They both felt instantaneous desire and feelings of intimacy for their respective objects of affection. Not unlike John's introduction to Rebecca, David's introduction to Daniella was fumbled.

Despite David's air of cockiness, Daniella, like his mother to his father, felt an unexpected attraction to and curiosity about David. Just as David's mom slipped her phone number to his father via the ticket, Daniella also gave her number to David in a nonthreatening way. Instead of writing her phone number down, however, Daniella simply said aloud to Nelson, "My Phone number is 555-LOVE (555-5683); give it to your friend there". She, then, coyly walked away with a slight finger wave to Nelson and never looked back.

On the way home, Nelson was excited about this exchange. He was not quite sure what it was all about, but instinctively knew it was important to David. Being a young male, albeit somewhat delayed, began teasing David. "Davie got a girlfriend. Davie got a girlfriend" he repeatedly taunted David. David experienced a cornucopia of emotions about this taunting. He was flattered that Daniella obviously wanted him to have her phone number and he was hopeful that Nelson's taunting was prophetic, but he was scared and annoyed that she had the power to tug at his heartstrings this way. She, nevertheless, stayed on his mind and the next day, he called her.

(Daniella)

Daniella could not believe she had fallen for that cocky, tired line-speaking idiot. Even as she spouted these derogatory comments in her head, however, she felt a warm glow in her chest and a smile on her face. Even more difficult to believe was she had actually given him her phone number in that obviously silly way—what was wrong with her??? She just knew he would not call—that type of guy never did; they just collected phone numbers to show off. Well, at least, she did not write it down for him—this was her only pride. All evening she found herself unable to concentrate on anything and would jump in anticipation each time the phone rang. David had not called by ten thirty p.m. so Daniella went to bed.

The next morning when the phone rang, Daniella was so sure it would not be David, she did not answer. She began her morning routine, which included a twenty-minute shower. When she got out of the shower, she noticed her answering machine blinking. She simply stared for a minute, but then decided to listen to the message. Much to her joy and nervousness, it was "Him"!! David mumbled he was sorry he missed her, but wondered if she would meet him at the arcade that afternoon. Daniella went into a frenzy, trying to decide what to wear. She did not want to appear like she was trying to look good for him, but she wanted to "knock his socks off" when he did see her. Needless to say, Daniella could not concentrate on any activity all day—she could only think about the impending meeting with David. Daniella realized David was probably younger than she was and this briefly caused her to reflect on why she seemed to always be attracted to younger guys.

At the age of fifteen, Daniella was usually described as a raving beauty; most persons who saw her viewed her this way. Of the Hispanic race, yet born and bred in America, she seemed to fit in both worlds. In fact, on the surface, Daniella appeared to have the perfect life. Her parents, who hailed from Honduras when they were very young, had become very successful here on American soil. They had their respective masters' degrees, were bi-lingual and owned their own businesses. Mr. Ramon Sanchez, Sr., (now known as Raymond) was very successful corporate raider. Mrs. Consuela Sanchez (now known as Connie) created and built up her own real estate business.

Yes, the Sanchez family looked picture-perfect. The façade, however, was exactly that—a façade. In reality, Daniella's mom was not the cultured, agreeable society bred lady she presented to the world; she actually was plagued with emotional problems and a need to control. Her father was very domineering and charismatic in his business ventures, but at home, he was extremely submissive. All of this, of course, occurred in the privacy of the home. In public, the Sanchezs were the ideal American family, despite being of the Hispanic heritage on American soil.

Not only were the Sanchezs not the ideal married couple, but they, also, were not the ideal parents. In public, they would boast about their children and have them dressed in what was considered befitting of their current social status. In private, however, the Sanchezs spent little, if any time, with Daniella and her brother, Ramon. In fact, Connie often belittled the kids and would ship them off to their grandparents as often as the grandparents would allow. The reasoning for them to visit with the grandparents always involved the mother stating they were unruly and she could not control them. As the grandparents aged and questioned what this unruly behavior, about which the mother made claims, were, the visits became fewer and further in between. Daniella and Ramon felt hurt by the parental claims, but they did enjoy going to the grandparents; when these visits slowed, thus, this was just one more piercing of the heart for Daniella.

After Mrs. Sanchez could no longer conveniently "ship" her children to their grandmother, she then began making bogus accusations to social and juvenile services. Since the Sanchezs were so upstanding in the community, no one questioned these accusations. If anything, they offered sympathy and a means to swiftly and privately swoop them through the system. Many of the society ladies would whisper how unfortunate it was that the Sanchezs were such wonderful parents, giving their children the best of opportunities and yet they (the children) did not appreciate it. That Ramon and Daniella were the most ungrateful children they had ever met. During periods of accusations, the Sanchez children would be removed and placed in foster homes, juvenile detention centers and sent to various agencies for counseling. Of course, while undergoing counseling, the parents did not have to deal with them. In fact, they would often take cruises, host charity balls and go on business trips without even checking in with the temporary quarters of their children.

Daniella would cringe when another false accusation of drug use, alcohol use, sexual promiscuity and pure obstinate behavior was made against her or her brother. Her self-esteem was practically nonexistent and she wondered why her parents disliked her and her brother so very much. When Daniella would be out of the home, she would experience relief and pain. Relief existed because she did not have to listen to the verbal battering of her mother and pain because she was fearful that persons may believe what her mother claimed about her. Occasionally, she would find foster parents or social workers that would listen to her and caused her to think that maybe someone really believed she was a person of worth. Ramon was so quiet and withdrawn about everything, Daniella never really knew how or if their parents and their lives affected him.

Daniella recalled many times how she would cringe when she would read newspaper articles about how the Sanchezs had made another major contribution to society through fund raising and their business acumen and successes. These were the same parents who would leave the home for weeks at a time. Raymond would go on extended business trips and upon his return, he and his wife would fight endlessly. Daniella and Ramon would often hear their mother yell at their father for "leaving her here with these little monsters". By the time Daniella was twelve, her mother had begun going on jaunts to "find herself". She would leave money there for twelve year old Daniella and fifteen year old Ramon to "fiend" for themselves. They were responsible for getting their own meals and to school (if they were not in foster homes or juvenile detention) It was this publicly fake life that resulted in Daniella being attracted to younger guys. Subconsciously, she felt she would not be as powerless and helpless. Interestingly enough, David too sought persons he felt he could dominate; yet, the two were oddly drawn to each other.

Daniella pulled herself from her dark thoughts and refocused on her excitement about seeing David later. Though deeply attracted to David, she hoped Nelson would be with him, too. This not only might protect her from getting too deeply involved too quickly, but she felt deep compassion for Nelson. Having survived the life she lived, she wanted to protect Nelson from the cruel world just as David did.

(David and Daniella)

Afternoon slowly, slowly eased its way into the day. David had been pacing and had been irritated all day. He kicked himself for the dumb message he left and he had no idea if she would really show. David decided to not let Nelson tag along in case Daniella did not show and Nelson asked too many questions. Just as he was building his protective wall behind a façade of potentially simmering anger, he sensed her presence. Without even looking up, his throat constricted and he began a silent mantra "Be cool, be cool, be cool". He tried to casually sway around so as to appear unaffected, but when he saw her, his breath caught in his throat. As before, instead of speaking words, he was again reduced to unintelligible mumbling.

Having chosen a red checkered midriff top, blue jean capris and red open toe shoes, Danielle had been full of self-confidence until she actually saw David. When she saw him, she questioned every decision she had made that day. David swaggered towards her and she heard a mumbled "whuz up?" Daniella breathed in deeply, responded with a shy hello and then without missing a beat, the two began chattering as if they had known each other forever.

David and Daniella played a few of the games in the Arcade and he was quite impressed how well she played some of the more aggressive games. They then sauntered to the Food Court portion of the Mall. He offered to pay for both of their McDonald combo meals, but Daniella insisted on paying for her own. David decided right then and there; he had to find a way to make money after school and in the summers. He did not know if there was any legitimate way for a thirteen-year old to make money, but he did not care. He would find a way to be able to pay to date Daniella. He could not wait until he was older to work and date Daniella for he did not want her to 'get away'.

Both of their minds were riddled with individual thoughts; yet, they had not ceased talking the whole time, even while competitively playing video games. What they talked about, neither could have said. They were simply happy to be in each other's company and were basking in the wonder of teenage first love flutters. David had been dropped at the Mall by his mom and knew it was about time to go. (It was a Friday afternoon and mom did not have to work that night). He asked Daniella if she needed a ride; she said no, but suggested they walk out together. Nothing could have prepared David for the next event. His mother was pulling up in their modest Chevrolet Celebrity when Daniella took out keys and started towards a cherry red Mustang Convertible. Shock and distress registered in his mind, body and limbs. Daniella had her own car and she was not even sixteen yet! How could he compete for her affections. She must be loaded. He was not even old enough for a driver's license. It then dawned on him that neither was she so if she was getting away with driving, maybe he could, too. On the drive home, David was very quiet trying to figure out how to handle this wrinkle. It was not a situation about which he could ask his mother—he would just have to think long and hard.

Still musing over how Daniella was able to have her own car and drive, David began to get twinges of anticipation, too. He thought of how he would be the envy of all of the boys in his town if he could be seen riding around with the gorgeous "older" woman in this phat car. Again, he thought Daniella might consider letting him drive her car. He would have to get more information from her. David pulled himself together and called her. He told her how much he enjoyed the afternoon and then ever so casually inquired about whose car that was and how she was able to drive it. Daniella, with what sounded like a twinge of frustration, explained her parents were trying to make up for some things they had done to her in the past. She said she would tell him about it one day, but to make a long story short, she said her parents pulled some strings, got her a hardship license and bought her that car. David said he would love to feel that wheel and engine under his hands. Since he now appeared older than thirteen, Daniella and David decided this was a feasible plan.

When David and Daniella hung up the phone, she was pleased with the conversation; so was he for a very brief moment, but then he had another startling thought. Daniella must be really rich and though this sent a thrill through him, fear also shot through his system. He did not have this type of money; he, in fact, had been thinking of some part time job earlier. If Daniella had this kind of money, would this make her the boss??? His father and uncle had always made it plain the man was to be in charge; that was the only way to be "the man". They had already shared that when he started dating, he should drive, pay the way and remain the one in charge of the relationship. This was not going well; Daniella was older (age 15), had her own car and it sounded as if had her own money. What had she meant about her parents trying to buy her off for the past and pulling strings for her to get the car??? David had much pondering in which to engage. Even with all of these distressing thoughts, the thirteen-year old male side resurfaced—what a thrill to be seen in that car. How cool to only be thirteen and have an older girlfriend and not need parents to take them to the movies, the mall, out to eat, etc. Besides, David could pass for sixteen. He was buff, large boned, muscular, almost as tall as his daddy and already showing signs of incoming facial hair. This was one area which could not be argued—David was a good looking guy and did appear older than his thirteen years.

Though David knew lots of people and had gotten in trouble with more than just a few, until now his only true blue friend had been Nelson. He had basically figured out in his mind that despite the obstacles, he would be with Daniella. His issue now was how to tell Nelson he would be spending more time with a girl without hurting him or losing his allegiance. David, also, wanted to find a way to incorporate Nelson into this new relationship. He did not want him to always be with them, of course, but he definitely wanted Daniella, Nelson and himself to be a triangle of some sort.

The relationship with Daniella and David became very serious very quickly. They were so young, others thought it was pure puppy love, but this was one of those rare couples that found each other when they were adolescents and really developed a long-term romance and friendship. As they spent more and more time talking on the phone, they knew they really wanted to see each other a lot, too. David's usual dilemma was how to work this in with his friendship with Nelson. Over the years, David had dropped many acquaintances because of how they treated Nelson. Thinking back to his meeting with Daniella, he was sure she would treat him well. After all, it was because she was helping Nelson that he himself met her. David, however, was still very protective of Nelson and found he was stressing over the situation. Finally, one day, he bit the bullet, told Daniella that he wanted the three of them to spend some time together. Much to his relief, she eagerly agreed. They made arrangements to meet at their usual spot (The Arcade) over the weekend.

Nelson was bouncing impatiently from foot to foot as David told him he needed to talk to him before going to the Arcade. David felt himself becoming angry at his childish behavior, but mentally reprimanded himself; told himself he was just nervous and to chill. Finally, he explained to Nelson that the reason he had spent less time with him recently was due to him spending time with a girl. He asked if he remembered the girl who had helped him with the machines at the arcade. Nelson blushed and giggled and said, "yea, Davie's girlfriend". David, good-naturedly, punched him in the arm and told him that her name was Daniella. He told him, as well, they would be spending time together today. Nelson grinned and nodded okay. Relief suffusing his body, David told Nelson to come on and they headed for the Arcade.

CHAPTER NINE

Summer

With pounding heart, David saw his dream standing next to their usual machine. The shocker, though, was there was someone else with her—a girl. This attractive, dimpled faced, brown skinned female with her long hair hanging down her back, was chatting animatedly to Daniella. When David sauntered over to them and was introduced to Summer Knight by Daniella, he noticed Nelson blushing furiously. Summer smiled and shook hands with Nelson. Daniella said Summer was one of her best friends. She was the daughter of one of the only social workers who had ever shown any trust in Daniella. Summer accepted Daniella for whom she was and was not the least stressed by what others said of her and thought of her. As David looked closer at this girl they called 'Summer", he was surprised at how pretty she actually was. She was so vibrant and up beat, one almost overlooked her physical beauty. He wondered if this triangle was going to turn into a foursome.

The four youths spent all afternoon together. Daniella and David would have moments of forgetting the others were there, but generally, they all participated in the conversation. Nelson was able to participate as well, though he was not as adept at communicating. Daniella and Summer, however, both had compassion for Nelson and they genuinely liked him. They, therefore, had no problems relating to him and including him in their group. Nelson obviously had a crush on Summer. He would stare at her and giggle on a frequent basis without provocation. Every time she looked at him, Nelson would blush furiously. Summer noticed, of course, but she never acted condescending towards him.

Summer had grown up with a mother for a social worker and her mother usually worked with the mentally ill and / or learning disabled population. Summer, thus, felt no self-consciousness with nor disdain towards Nelson. She accepted him for whom he was. This was the first person, excluding David, who had done this for Nelson. Nelson, being thirteen chronologically, felt the first stirrings of hormones. He felt self-conscious, yet a warm glow for Summer. The four, thus, had a wonderful time talking, eating and eventually, going to the movies.

(Summer Knight)

Summer was the daughter of divorced parents. Her mother was a social worker and her father was a high school principal. She had only been six when they divorced. Summer was unusual though in that she did not feel victimized by the divorce. She still had contact with both parents though she had chosen to live with her mom. Summer was a cheerful, happy go lucky young lady. She did not focus on the bad times because she enjoyed being happy too much. When she met Daniella and learned of her home life, Summer felt grateful her parents divorced instead of having her live that kind of life.

Summer had actually met Daniella accidentally. Having to leave school early one day due to being ill, her mom had picked her up on her way to meet with Daniella in juvenile. Summer went with her and even with her runny nose, red-rimmed eyes and sore throat, she took an immediate liking to Daniella. Daniella was so pretty, while looking so sad. Having a sunny disposition and wanting everyone else to feel good, too, Summer had tried to reassure Daniella that everything would be okay; she told her, her mom would help her. Daniella had been very despondent; however, Summer's reassurance and insistence that life could be good became contagious to her that day. Mrs. Knight had listened to Daniella's story, worked some magic neither Daniella nor Summer ever understood and had taken Daniella away from juvenile and home with them that night. That was five years ago when the girls were ten. To this day, Daniella spent many days in the Knight home. This is why Daniella had been so anxious for David to meet Summer.

When the afternoon ended, David felt regret and sadness. This time of his life was one of the happiest he had remembered since before his mother miscarried his baby brother. Even though it had been over eight years, David still felt tears behind his eyes and a lump in his throat as he thought about the loss of the brother he never knew. He sometimes wondered if this is why he cared so much about Nelson. David had engaged in many escapades as he had thought of doing so many years ago.

In fact, David recalled only a year ago one of the pranks he and Nelson had pulled. He remembered one Wednesday evening during a school break, Nelson's grandmother had invited David to spend the night with Nelson. She had gone to Bible Study and had left the boys at home. She had left them money to order pizza. David and Nelson had ordered pizza, but kept the money. What they did, was use the vacant adjoining apartment in the duplex in which Nelson and his grandmother lived. Several weeks prior, when the neighbors moved, the boys had found a way to get in and out of the apartment without being discovered. This night, they called for pizza and ordered it for the apartment next door. When they saw the pizza deliverer arriving, David slipped out the back door of Nelson's and went in through the back of the adjoining apartment. When the guy knocked on the door, David answered, took the pizza and told him he would have to get money from "mom". David shut the door behind him and ran next door to Nelson's. He and Nelson were doubled over in giggles when there was a knock at Nelson's door. Nelson answered and there stood the delivery guy, wanting to know if Nelson knew the Smiths (pseudo name David had given) next door. Nelson, with a look of innocence, said the apartment next door was empty. The pizza delivery guy was furious and said he would call the cops. He called from his cell phone and when the police arrived, they questioned Nelson at the door. One of the uniformed officers saw David lurking in the background. He immediately became suspicious that David was involved. When he checked, however, there were no neighbors next door; the boys had hidden the pizza. The delivery guy did not see David in the house and could not identify Nelson, so they had to let it drop. They advised the guy he had "been taken", but they had insufficient evidence of how or by whom. Nelson and David again broke into gales of laughter when everyone was gone. They pocketed the money for a later trip to the Arcade and David felt pride within himself that he once again "***ruled!***"

Now though he wanted to do better, be better for Daniella. David felt his chest constrict as he became aware of how much he cared for Daniella. This was so very apparent to him when he thought of how vivacious and pretty Summer was; yet, he felt no attraction to her. David had eyes for one person and one person only—Daniella. As he was wallowing in his mixture of emotions about feeling such love for Daniella, responsibility for Nelson and wanting to be so much better, he suddenly brightened. The four young persons already had plans to meet up again in a couple of days. This should keep him going and besides, he could always talk to Daniella in the meantime.

(David)

As David became more and more involved with Daniella and their little group of friends, his juvenile delinquent tendencies took a nosedive. Though he did not completely give them up, he did engage in them less and less. Some of this was due to lack of time; some of it because he was more interested in other things and some of it due to his maturing. Whereas before, David engaged in deviant behaviors to feel powerful, now he did it primarily to obtain things he wanted or felt he needed and did not have the money for them. Much of his theft involved getting gifts for Daniella. She was at the center of his every thought.

Before changing some of his behaviors, David had already developed a reputation for being "a problem". This would haunt him longer than he could ever imagine. Over the years, David had perfected his shoplifting skills. He had learned how to be successful at the fine art of being able to pick pocket. Not only had he pulled antics at school on his teachers and classmates, but he had also engaged in community vandalism. In fact, he recalled one act of vandalism that he was now mature enough to recognize as being both 'mean and dangerous'. Halloween seemed to be his pick, as it was for many, to engage in vandalism. One Halloween, he, Nelson and some of his 'in school suspension boys', had spent much of the night going from one street to the next using pay phones. They would call for taxi service and when the taxis arrived, they would throw eggs at the car and then disappear behind houses where they could not be detected. David had been questioned time and time again by the "men in blue" as well as by his school principal, the school truancy officer, store security guards, his parents and numerous other adults. No one, nevertheless, had ever been able to prove David was behind the antics and/or had committed the crimes. This had only served to cause David to feel more invincible and powerful. Though this need was still deep within him, he had less need to engage in deviant antics due to feeling admired and loved by Daniella and his group of friends. He, however, could not fully cease his deviant behavior and the future would still be sporadically riddled with these behaviors.

CHAPTER TEN

The Victim

It was Christmas time and David's mom was short of money. She decided to obtain a small, short-term loan from a Kwik Kash company. Needless to say, the lines were long and so David became very restless as they waited. Just as his mind began wandering, he noted an apparently unhappy woman standing in line ahead of him. He became very amused just listening to the ranting and raving of this female.

(Cherie)

Cherie', a fifty-five year old, graying Bi-racial female was very angry and it was obvious even to David, that she was not comfortable in her own skin. Cherie' had the coloring of a mulatto and the stereotyped attitude/ behavior of a ghetto resident. Based upon her dress, it was assumed she leaned towards her black heritage in that she wore African garb and wore her hair wavy and closely cropped her head. Cherie' was almost stamping her feet as she complained to the loan officer that she needed much more than the $75 they were offering her.

Furious, Cherie began thinking to herself that she could not believe she was again in this type of situation. Her life began scrolling before her eyes like clips from a home movie. She first recalled the pain immersing her as she folded her little body as far back in the corner of her bedroom as possible more than forty years earlier. Tears had streamed from her large brown eyes and rushed down her face like a fountain that had no end. Even within her memories, she remembered the taste of blood as she bit her lip to prevent the animal wailing from escaping. Rocking back and forth like a wounded animal, she stressed over how this could have happened to her. She had always tried to be the good little obedient girl who did the right things. Her only desires in life were to have a father to protect her, a mother to befriend her, family dinners at night and a boyfriend to shower her with love. Now, here she was at fourteen, feeling not happiness and anticipation of true love, but contemplating suicide.

Cherie was an only child. She resided with her mother and for the past six years, her stepfather. Though Cherie's stepfather had adopted her, she never felt love and warmth from him. She believed he tolerated her simply because of her mother. Mrs. Robinson went through the motions of being the right kind of mother. She made sure Cherie had clothing, school supplies, shelter and food. Even with the food, however, her mom was always admonishing her to watch what she ate so she would not get fat. If she got fat, no man would want her. Mrs. Robinson told Cherie she would need a man to "take care of her" so she had to do whatever was necessary to attract him. She, also, told her she would have a hard time finding this person since she was "mixed" and therefore, she had to be extra careful with her appearance if she wanted to attract Mr. Right. In reality, all Cherie really desired was a father.

Cherie's father, as had been told to her, deserted her mother when he found out her mother was pregnant with her. Her mother used to be a risk taker and defied all societal rules. Her biggest act of defiance was to date a Caucasian. This was really defiance at the time since Cherie was conceived in 1944. From Mrs. Robinson's stories, she had really loved this guy and had been convinced he loved her. When she first learned she was pregnant, she had pictured him rescuing her from her lower middle class life, loving her and helping her raise their beautiful child. Instead of this fairy tale ending, her father had turned tail and acted as if he had never even known her mom. He, in fact, married within a week of learning of the pregnancy. He told her mother they were "just having fun"; that he was marrying the daughter of a family friend. Their families had business connections and it had always been understood they would marry. He told her to never contact him again and if she tried to make trouble, to remember "no one in Mississippi would believe the accusations of a little colored girl over the denial of an upstanding White male citizen". It was then Mrs. Robinson left her rural Mississippi town and fled to Tennessee for a fresh start. Once arriving and settling in Tennessee, she told everyone she was a young widow. Needless to say, this was not the most auspicious beginning of Cherie's life. From that point on, in one way or another, she had believed she was to blame for her mother's loss of dreams. Even her mom met her stepfather and married him when Cherie was eight, nothing changed. Cherie still did not have the family she desired.

Seeking approval, Cherie would work hard at her appearance, deny herself foods she craved, always be quiet in the presence of her stepfather and offer help with the home to her mother. Because of her bi-racial heritage, she had the characteristics of both races and was quite attractive. She thus, began attracting attention from males. Cherie, naively, believed this attention was due to love—not lust.

When a twenty-two year old showed an interest in her, she thought she must really be special. Here was an older male, who unlike her father, wanted her. He would call her over to his little store that he owned, when she would be walking home from school, ask about her day; tease her about boyfriends and tell her if he was younger, she would be his. Cherie was so flattered and dreamt one day she would be old enough for him. Several weeks later after these after school talks, he told her he was closing the store early and asked if she would like to go to the neighborhood park. Cherie was not sure her mother would approve, but knew her mother would not be home for at least two hours. She, thus, acquiesced. Much to her horror, after arriving there, he began touching her private parts. When she shrunk back, he became hostile, pulled her behind a dumpster in the back of the sheltered pavilions, tore her underclothes and raped her. He then left her on the ground, trying in vain to control her sobbing and to pull her tattered clothing around her. Cherie withdrew and began taking a different route home from school. Now, five weeks later, she had discovered she was pregnant.

"Mrs. Miller, Mrs. Miller!" David wondered if she was going to answer the loan officer or just keep looking off into space. "Mrs. Miller, do you want the money available? If so, we need to complete the paperwork". It suddenly registered with Cherie that the loan officer was talking to her. She had been so caught up in her reverie, she had not recognized her married name when he called it. This calling out to her almost slammed her back to her memories of being a scared fourteen-year old girl. Movie clips of her life began scrolling back again to the place where she was hearing, "Cherie, Cherie, do you want the abortion? If so, we need to complete the proper forms and do the pre-procedure counseling".

Upon learning of the positive results of her pregnancy test, Cherie's initial thought was there was no way she could actually have this baby. That would require her to face her mother whom she could never ever face with this in a million years. Cherie could not deal with this humiliation of what she perceived as her fault nor could she give up her dreams of meeting "Mr. Right". She had sought the assistance of a crisis pregnancy center where she did not have to be of age, to receive service. Now, however, sitting in this cold, gray, dreary cinder blocked, impersonal office, second thoughts began stirring within her. Was she just like her biological father? Was she turning her back on this innocent baby even before it was born just as her biological father had done to her and her mother? Cold chills rushed down her back and her heart was gripped with fear as if in a tight vise. No matter the circumstances or consequences, there was no way Cherie could abort something/someone that was a part of her. She fled the building and went home to attempt to build her courage to tell her mother.

Sitting stiffly on the hard kitchen floor, Cherie was overcome by brief blindness. Feeling faint, she slightly swayed, but then called "Mama". At least, she thought she had called out to her mother, but her mother did not answer. She thought she croaked out "Mama" again, but realized this calling out to her mother was only in her mind. No words had actually left her lips. Wetting her parched lips with her tongue, twirling strands of her hair and mentally gathering all of her strength and courage, she firmly called out to her mother one more time. This time the sound actually whistled through her lips and her mother turned from washing the dishes to see Cherie crossing and uncrossing her legs. Her first response was "Stop that fidgeting! Smooth your hair and sit up straight in that chair. Now, what do you want???" Cherie tried to respond, but was so nauseated and faint, she could barely hold her head up and form the words that were strangling in her throat. Finally, finally, she was able to softly stutter, "I-I am preg-preg-pregnant".

The next scene moved in slow motion—Cherie was expecting her mother to be upset, but nothing prepared her for the horrifying speech her mother was vomiting. "You're what? Girl, don't you play with me!! I didn't sacrifice my life to raise a whore." Cherie stared open mouthed in total disbelief. Had her mother forgotten that Cherie herself was born out of wedlock??? Cherie actually briefly blacked out and when she regained consciousness, her mother was still spewing venom at her. Mrs. Robinson never even noticed the fear, horror and the illness that her only daughter was experiencing. She was too busy lamenting about her sacrifices, the shame Cherie had brought on her and Mr. Robinson and how this would affect her life. She never even asked Cherie about the father, acting as if this was something Cherie had to have done strictly on her own. She was screaming obscenities at her and something about her being a half-breed, low life whore that no decent man would ever look at, want or marry!!!

As the hurtful emotional darts were being hurled at her, Cherie was suddenly able to snap out of her swirling cesspool of pain when she heard the statement: "Your real daddy would be so disappointed in you if he knew. I thank God he does not know". Cherie felt anger pierce her heart, soul and mind. How dare her mother allude to the bastard who had deserted her and her mom. Why she was acting as if he was someone respectable and special. If it was not for him, she nor her mother would be in their current situations. Without thinking and for the first time in her life, Cherie got a backbone. She stood up literally and figuratively to her mother and began spewing venomous words and accusations at her. Mrs. Robinson slapped Cherie so hard, her head snapped back. Mrs.

Robinson then, unexpectedly slumped down on a chair and wept. Cherie recovering from the anger and the slap, was sick with guilt. She, rather awkwardly, put her arms around her mother and tried to comfort her.

What happened next would forever live in Cherie's mind. Her mother, who was usually so harsh and judgmental, seemed to shrink before Cherie's very eyes. She became softer, turned to Cherie, pulled her onto her lap and into her warm embrace and repeatedly said "I'm sorry, I'm sorry. I really do love you, I love you, baby". She then rocked her back and forth, crooned into her ears, smooth her hair and was the mother Cherie had always dreamt of. The scared little fourteen-year old mother-to-be sank into the arms and warmth of her mother's arms. Hope surfaced and Cherie thought there might be some chance that she finally had the mother she wanted as she herself was embarking on the threshold of motherhood. Cherie thought briefly that maybe she could tell her mother that she was actually raped.

These sweet dreams were short lived as Cherie's stepfather walked in and shattered this bittersweet moment. He boomed "What's wrong with you simpering broads?" When Mrs. Robinson shared Cherie's predicament, her stepfather dryly retorted that he had always known she would be a little slut. He told her mother he had told her she should have gotten rid of the brat at birth. Stunned and speechless, Cherie once again felt faint when her mother did not defend her nor reprimand her stepfather. Instead, she simply pushed Cherie off of her lap, stood up, went back to the kitchen sink to finish the forgotten dishes and asked her husband what he wanted for dinner. In a twinkling of an eye, the brief illusive maternal instinct Cherie so craved and had for a brief moment, dissipated. Cherie never revealed the truth about the rape and her mother never questioned the paternity of the child.

The next seven months of Cherie's pregnancy were miserable. Her mother treated her as if she did not exist and when her stepfather would speak to her, he always alluded to "sluttish behavior of teens". Cherie tried to stay out of everyone's way. She dropped out of school for the duration of her pregnancy and basically, felt like a pariah. Cherie had no idea what to expect from delivery and never knew if her stages of pregnancy were within normal realms/expectations. She, naturally, was afraid and unhappy throughout pregnancy. Surprisingly, when she did go into labor, her mother went with her to the hospital and remained for the fifteen-hour labor and delivery. Finally after mind boggling, almost unbearable pain Cherie had ever felt, her seven pound, two ounce, wailing, squirming baby boy was born. Immediately upon delivery, Cherie felt an alien, unexpected, overwhelming love for this helpless little person in her arms. She decided there was hope that someone loved her for her—her baby boy!! In the very near future, she also learned that her mother was a much better grandmother than she was a mother. Though she would always grieve the lack of the mother she desired, she was happy that at least her son had a caring grandmother.

At first, Cherie absolutely basked in the love and care her mother showered upon baby Nicholas. She saw her mother attend to Nicholas like she herself had never experienced from mom. As the weeks grew into months, Cherie began to feel she was in competition for Nicholas' affection. He seemed to prefer her mother over her and Cherie once again developed that sense of being unloved, unneeded and just a burden to everyone. She focused all of her energies in school where she had resumed attendance after the birth of the baby. She excelled academically, but still did poorly socially. The boys all chased her because she was so attractive, but once they dated her, they never called back. Becoming aware that she had a baby and as her low self-esteem would bleed through, most guys would run out of fear. This, of course, just fed into Cherie's poor self-image and her budding thought processes of how unfair life was to her. In spite of her flailing social life, by the end of her senior year in high school, she had met Jacob Miller. Jacob, a stockily built, fairly short, chocolate brown male, should have by all rights, really feared Cherie. He, however, showed no fear and approached her boldly. He told her how he liked her bi-racial heritage, but taught her how he thought an African American Princess (as he called her) should walk, act and think. Cherie bought right into it. It was because of Jacob, in fact, that she presently wore African style dress and current hairstyle.

By this point, David had grown bored and weary with watching this lady and her antics. He was glad she finally took the $75, stopped having a tantrum and stopped getting that occasional far away look she kept having in her eyes. What he did not know was this moment in time had triggered so many painful memories for Cherie and indeed, had validated further for her that she would always be a victim. In fact, at that very minute, Cherie was fuming over what she viewed as the 'white man's oppression' of her. She knew she deserved much more out of life, but decided she would never make it, never be accepted and never be good enough in the white man's world. She never considered her own attitude and response to life might have been the problem.

(Cherie & Jacob)

Floods and floods of memories overwhelmed Cherie. As she prepared to leave the loan company, her mind was still churning with other forms of her personal victimization.

Cherie's mind resumed its recounting of her meeting with Jacob. For the first time in what seemed to her to be forever, she felt someone loved her. Cherie finished school a year late due to having taken time to give birth to a baby, but this, she had decided, was a blessing in disguise. This gave her more time to get to know Jacob who was a year younger than her. They graduated together and for Cherie this served as a bond of cement for them. This had to be fate. After all, she had only met him because she had been out a year and thus, was now a year behind in school.

The first eighteen years of her life had been hard, but she was on her way. Throughout her and Jacob's senior year, the couple was almost inseparable. During the day, Jacob would walk Cherie to her various classes and they always ate lunch together. At night, he would call her or come over and spend time with her and the baby. Her mother initially acted happy about the relationship, but she eventually began voicing displeasure. She would remind Cherie that she was a mother and did not have the right to have a social life like other teens. Cherie would let this influence her thinking and behavior and she would withdraw from Jacob and begin snapping short retorts to his compliments of her. Jacob, nonetheless, would not back off. He, actually, would smile at her, tell her she was beautiful when angry and express emotional support for her turmoil. Cherie felt torn as if betraying her mom by listening to Jacob, but she would still allow him to lull her back to a mental pasture of contentment and peace.

Baby Nicholas was growing and becoming attached to Jacob as well. At times, he would call him daddy, which only irritated Cherie's mother further. She would make snide comments about how no one would believe this child was the product of Cherie and Jacob. She said he did not look like a half-breed as Cherie did and was. Cherie would usually drop her head, allow these words to ferment in her subconscious and then spend the rest of the evening proving she was a dedicated mother. She would not return Jacob's calls and if he came over, tell him he needed to leave. She would then cry herself to sleep. The next day, predictable as a Swiss watch, Jacob would be waiting for her and would validate she was a person of worth. This consistency on his part eventually won Cherie over to him. Though her mom's words cut her to the heart like sharpened knife, Jacob's words were the anesthesia to alleviate the pain. By the end of the school year, Cherie and Jacob plans for marriage.

Mrs. Robinson voiced disapproval and reminded Cherie, Jacob could not possibly really love someone like her; she told her no decent man would take another man's baby to raise, forgetting her own husband had taken in Cherie. Mrs. Robinson pounded and pounded at Cherie for days on end. Cherie had begun developing a spine though and she let what she saw with Nicholas and Jacob and what she heard from Jacob influence her the most. When Mrs. Robinson saw she had "lost", she mentally declared the battle lost, not the war. She changed her tactics and began giving support, helping Cherie plan the wedding. She even allowed Cherie and Jacob to have the ceremony at her home.

On her wedding day, Cherie felt she was floating in heaven. After two years, Jacob was still here and Nicholas was a happy, healthy five-year old kindergarten student. Cherie had it all: a high school diploma, a man who loved her, student loans to go to college and a tiny apartment called home. She was going to prove to her biological father, wherever he was, that she had not needed him after all. She hoped one day to run into the no good monster who had raped her so he could see she did not need him either. Her storybook life had begun. The only cloud hanging over her life was when her mother whispered sinisterly to her to "not get too comfortable with Jacob; to remember she could always bring Nicholas back home and to never fully move everything she owned into the home of a man". When Cherie had protested that this was her home, too, her mother simply replied, "he is a man and you will have to learn this the hard way". This gnawed at the recesses of Cherie's consciousness at the most unexpected moments. What did this mean? It was so contradictory to mom's advice years earlier that she would "need a man to take care of her". It, however, affected her responses to Jacob. When she would think this way, she would act in a distant, cool way that would actually cause Jacob to emotionally move away from her over time. This almost indecipherable moving away only validated that her mother may have been known some secret Cherie did not know. She had no idea she was actually pushing Jacob away.

Cherie, nevertheless, went to college; Nicholas went to kindergarten and Jacob went to work. Jacob truly loved Nicholas, but he began to feel used/abused when Cherie left more and more of the parenting to him because "she had to study". She would expect Jacob to 'pick up the slack' with the housework and childcare. He had no problem with doing his share, but he became frustrated when he realized Cherie only studied and complained there was 'never enough money'. He found he was the one financially supporting the family, planning the meals or at least, picking them up from fast food places and making sure Nicholas had his homework completed, clean clothes and supplies for school. When he approached Cherie about this, she immediately launched into how she should have listened to her mother. She would then go to her mom's house for several days at a time, taking "her baby" with her. She would remind Jacob how he was not the father and she did not need a "pity marriage". She would turn from her African heritage and remind him she was better than him because she was half white. Jacob would be completely baffled, hurt and then soon thereafter, began responding with isolation or angry words. When Cherie would run home, her mom would welcome her with open arms and encourage her to leave some of hers and Nicholas' possessions each time she went back home. It never dawned on Cherie how mom had never been supportive of her before and she forgot how she used to crave the support, warm hugs and kind words from mom. Because she did not think through this, she did not realize how foreign this behavior was for her mom. She never questioned the motives; just began blaming Jacob for "failing her".

Jacob was flabbergasted at how short-lived his honeymoon was. Cherie used to boast about physical intimacy being a God given gift and how she wanted to always be beautiful and desirable to her husband. She used to take bubble baths, light scented candles, take Nicholas to her mom some weekends so the two of them could be alone and talk about wanting to have a baby with Jacob. Now she called him a chauvinist pig when he alluded to the desire for romance or started to question why he was Mr. Mom and breadwinner. Cherie would tell him she was a person and not a toy for him. Jacob would stare at her as if trying to see what was going on inside her head. He had never wanted to or thought he had treated his African princess like a nonentity. The arguments would ensue long into the night and Nicholas soon started acting up and acting out. He cried frequently, fought the other kids at school and was disobedient to the teachers. Instead of Cherie seeing this as a product of his home environment, she first blamed the "white" teachers and then told Jacob he was modeling poor male behavior for "their son". Jacob would always be taken off guard by her one hundred eighty degree explanations. He never knew if she was going to blame the white man and be a poor black female or blame the no good black man and be above him because she was bi-racial. He never wanted to come home anymore; was tired of footing all the financial responsibility and did not understand why after three years of school, Cherie was still a first semester sophomore. He ceased inquiring though because this only led to more fights, silent treatments, a disturbed child and then eventually, the jaunts and overnight stays by Cherie and Nicholas to her mom's.

Jacob, as is often human nature, felt isolated, manipulated, depressed and angry by his wife's erratic behaviors. When his shapely, soft-spoken, intelligent, single, twenty-six year old female co-worker started being "available to listen" to him, he took advantage of it. Rhonda was so beautiful and unlike Cherie, she already had a college degree, was full of self-confidence and was only black. He, thus, did not have to worry about her 'studying', swinging from one race to the next or clinging to him with insecurities. The relationship began innocently enough. It led to Jacob feeling like he was not a bad person like he felt with Cherie. It caused him to avoid home even more and then finally, to look forward to Cherie running home to mom. Jacob had also noticed more and more items gradually disappearing from his apartment when Cherie left, but he was too emotionally spent and beat up by her now, to even care enough to inquire. Jacob fantasized about Rhonda when Cherie was berating him and he took every opportunity to be in

Rhonda's presence. The affair inevitably started. Instead of this leading to Jacob being angrier and more withdrawn at home, became more peaceful, more contented with doing the housework and happier to spend time with Nicholas. This served only to anger Cherie more. She, of course, ran to mom, her newfound support system and confidante.

Mrs. Robinson told her the "no good scum" was bound to be having an affair. She advised her to drop a class without telling him and use this time to "check up on him". She, also, advised Cherie to start keeping back part of the grocery money for herself and start her own account. Cherie, not only did not question this, she did not even consider the fact that her mother's marriage died long ago and she and her stepfather lived as co-habiting strangers. Cherie did not question where all of this support had been when she was young and needed love and mothering. She just sped full speed ahead with mom's advice. She even took it a step further and began pinching money from bill money Jacob gave her. When the late notices on credit card bills, car payments, rent and utility bills began arriving, Cherie told Jacob he never made enough-he was not a real man. When they were evicted from their home, Cherie had discovered evidence of the affair by then and she told Jacob if he had been working instead of running around with "fluff", this would not have happened. The marriage deteriorated more and more and Jacob did not even bother to deny the affair; he simply requested a divorce. Jacob had anticipated Cherie would jump at the opportunity of marital dissolution and run home to mom. Was he ever surprised when she said "absolutely not". She told Jacob this was a lifetime commitment and he had better get used to it. She told him he had better find and buy them a home, help her get through school and it was time for them to have a baby together. Jacob was amazed as he watched Cherie turn into the domineering woman her mom was when it suited her, but be a helpless victim when this was better suited for her needs.

Despite the reaction, Jacob viewed it as just that—a reaction. He did not cease the affair and figured as seldom as he and Cherie engaged in husband and wife duties, there would not be a chance of a baby coming. He decided to cool his heels and abide his time. He was straightforward with his lover, tried to settle into some routine and went on about his business.

Jacob could have been knocked over with a feather when Cherie acted really kind and sweet one night and made the announcement that she was "pregnant". Jacob received this news with a mixture of horror and wonderment. The horror was he knew this meant he would not be able to leave Cherie for Rhonda. The wonderment was that maybe Cherie was actually pregnant with someone else's child. Then he remembered an incident six weeks prior. It had been a routine night: he walked in the door from work—Cherie yelled at him for being late. He spent time with Nicholas—Cherie criticized him for being childish. He attempted to watch television, but Cherie kept nagging him and making demands about spending time with her. Jacob finally succumbed to alcohol to blunt the emotional pain and to tune out the ear piercing yammering. The next thing he remembered was awaking the next morning with Cherie lying next to him with a sneaky grin on her face. When he inquired about her smirking, she had only responded with "I told you this marriage was not over; I knew you still wanted me". She then hopped out of bed, sashayed to the bathroom and had treated him as a pariah from that time until now. He had to conclude there must have been sexual contact and he was the father; furthermore, he decided, no sober man in his right mind would be with Cherie. A cloud of sadness suffused his mind and body at that point.

Over the next few months, Jacob sank further and further into despondency while Cherie behaved as if the two of them were America's Sweetheart Couple. Cherie did not really behave warmly and kindly towards Jacob, but she did present well outwardly. Outsiders thought the Millers were so fortunate. To them, the Millers had succeeded in making the blending of families work and now they had a new baby on the way. Cherie physically blossomed and became more maternal. She spent more time with Nicholas and even engaged in the more traditional feminine family role. She began having dinner ready when Jacob came home; kept the home clean and neat and made sure Nicholas was completing his homework. Even Nicholas' teachers commented on how much better his behavior and work were. Jacob was glad for Nicholas that Cherie was nicer, but he knew deep within this was to 'punish him'.

Rhonda was still kind to Jacob and voiced support, but he noted she had begun dating other men. She told him since he and Cherie were reconciling, this was only fair to her. Jacob knew this was only fair to her, but he also knew he was not reconciled to Cherie in any manner outside the legal. He tried to explain this to Rhonda, but of course, all she saw was a very pregnant wife to whom Jacob went home nightly. Their relationship began to deteriorate and Cherie gloated as she noted Jacob looking sadder. As she shared this with her mother, she validated for her that Jacob had probably let the little floozie go and now they could be a family. She told Cherie to ignore his temporary state of sadness; this would go away and Cherie could keep her husband. Mrs. Robinson told Cherie since she had ignored her advice in the past about men, she was happy to see Cherie finally taking control of her family; maybe, all of her sacrifices for Cherie had not been completely in vain. Cherie was not so sure, but she felt more in control now that Jacob came home nightly. He and she did not really talk a lot, but she did not care-he was home where she could watch him.

As the pregnancy came to term, Jacob was almost suicidal. He knew within his heart of hearts, Cherie had not changed. He anticipated becoming "Mr. Mom" again and knew this time he would not even have the support of Rhonda. When Cherie went into labor late one rainy, stormy night, Jacob thought how appropriate that the outside weather mirrored his inside emotions.

The healthy baby girl was born without incident. The only surprise for Jacob was the unexpected overwhelming emotions he felt for this soft, light brown skinned, wrinkled baby with eyes that appeared much too knowing and clear for a newborn. Jacob loved Nicholas and had no idea he could feel anything deeper than he did for him, but he did. He felt a love that surpassed the love he used to have for Cherie, the love he had for Nicholas, and even the love he felt for Rhonda. It did not lessen his love for Nicholas and Rhonda, but it was a completely different experience. His stormy emotions began to subside and for the first time in years, he felt some inward peace.

When Cherie first noted Jacob's response to baby Celeste, she was thrilled, feeling this gave her even more control over him. He would never stray again. As the family, however, settled into a routine, Cherie felt a loss of control again. She returned to school; Nicholas was thrilled with his little sister and was now old enough to sort of have a little social life himself. She liked the aforementioned, but she hated the change in Jacob. He did resume household chores, spending time with Nicholas; would come straight home from work; seemed less depressed and was even making more money so their financial situation was better. What irritated Cherie was Jacob's obvious lack of feeling for her and his unconditional love for Celeste. He would walk around the house doing chores with Celeste on one hip and Nicholas simply following and talking with him animatedly. It was as if these two children were his and his only. Jacob acted as if the three of them had some sort of intimate relationship that did not involve her (Cherie). When she complained to mom, mom gave the caustic response that she just needed to be glad he was not out with floozies.

The Millers continued to appear to the world that they had a happy marriage and family. Both of the older Millers knew this was so untrue; their marriage was devoid of love and companionship. Nicholas had adjusted to the dysfunctional family and seemed settled in being "big brother" and spending time with Jacob when not on the phone or outside with his own little friends. Celeste, being the innocent, simply began growing up as 'daddy's girl'. Cherie became more infuriated as the rest of her family became more content.

Jacob desperately missed his relationship with Rhonda so he basked in the ability to have a friendship with her at work. He took some inward pleasure in the fact that when Celeste was turning five years of age, he still worked with Rhonda and she was still single. It began to stir a flicker of hope within him.

As Celeste entered kindergarten, Nicholas was turning thirteen. Jacob began to wonder if maybe the kids were old enough for him to seek a life on his own. He had adopted Nicholas; had a good relationship with him and had no fear of losing him should he and Cherie divorce. In addition, he had been the primary caregiver of Celeste since Cherie basically spent her time as a career student. He hinted around to Rhonda of his still ever present love for her, his lack of intimate life with Cherie and his thoughts of starting his own life. Rhonda was cautiously encouraging in this. Jacob, thus, would throw out little feelers to Celeste how she would feel if he and mom no longer lived together, but she still saw both of them. Being in this present world, Celeste had classmates who did this and thought nothing else of it. The Millers, behind closed doors, had never been a family since her birth anyway. When Jacob approached Nicholas and he responded in a careless teenage manner of "go for it", he knew the time had come to approach Cherie.

Jacob chose a weekend to discuss his plans with Cherie. This way, Nicholas was out with friends and Celeste was at a friend's slumber party. When he asked Cherie that morning if maybe they could have dinner together that night, she was suspicious, but then decided Jacob was "finally coming around". That night she dressed in a seductive manner, put her schoolbooks away and actually had a candlelight dinner ready for Jacob's arrival from work.

Jacob walked into a candlelit room with soft music playing, the scent of potpourri and a soft, feminine looking Cherie. This scared him spitless since he knew this meant she had a total different scenario planned than he did. He made a mental note to do no drinking, despite the deeply felt need for alcohol. He did not want to repeat this scene in five more years, only with there possibly being a new addition to the family. This was going to be much, much harder than he anticipated. He dreaded the wrath of Cherie when she learned the reason he wanted this dinner.

As Jacob showered and gathered his courage, Cherie sat smugly waiting his entrance. She would show her mom that she was still in control and Jacob did still want and love her despite the problems of the past few years. She did not think he had any other affairs after Rhonda; he was totally love with Celeste and though this attention had frustrated and angered her on numerous occasions, she decided this might have been a blessing in disguise.

After all, the two of them could only have conceived this child. Cherie had high hopes all was going well.

When Jacob sat down for dinner, he avoided Cherie's eyes throughout her chitchat. She rattled on about school and how great it was going. Jacob thought to himself how could it be anything, but great—that's all she had done for years while he provided for the family emotionally, financially and socially. As she continued to rattle and act as if this was a wonderful night, he felt the old frustrations surfacing and totally lost his nervousness. He actually interrupted her boring monologue with a blunt "I am filing for a divorce". He had meant to ask for a divorce; discuss Cherie's thoughts and feelings, but instead just bluntly stated his plans. Cherie stared in stun wonderment initially and then she went ballistic. She was sick of all of these people who were supposed to love her, betraying her: her biological father, her mother, her stepfather, Nichola's father and even her own children. Now here he biggest betrayer of them all was divorcing her. She should have left him years ago when he was sleeping around with that girl. She had given him the best years of her life and she was trying to better herself by becoming educated. NO, he would not leave her. She ranted and raved and then she picked up bowl of pasta, hit him over the head with it and told him to not hold his breath for this divorce. The glass bowl broke; thus, Jacob stood there with blood streaming down his face as well as pasta and Alfredo sauce. He shook his head in disbelief, but did not lose his resolve. He, in fact, moved out that night.

It had been difficult getting in to see the kids, getting a court date and getting joint custody of his children. He spent a lot of money, took a lot of harassment from Cherie and survived the onslaught of accusations that he had been abusive to Cherie. She had even insinuated he had unnatural affection for their daughter. After a long, hard year of attorneys, court, police investigations and more money than he could afford, Jacob was finally free of Cherie. He did indeed get joint custody of his kids and much to his pleasant surprise, they appeared fairly unscathed by the past year. He was now seeing Rhonda a lot and both of his children loved her. He wanted to marry her immediately, but knew he needed time to grieve and recover from his marriage to Cherie. He, also, wanted to make sure the kids were okay despite the outward appearance that they were. Eventually, he got back on his feet and was able to go on with his life.

Cherie, on the other hand, did not recover. She felt this validated even more the fact that everyone was against her. Her mother changed back from her support system to always saying "I told you so". Her kids seemed to prefer Jacob's company and she still was not out of school. She had fought hard to get alimony and child support, but that quack of a judge said it seemed Jacob had always been the primary caregiver for the kids. He said Jacob should have the kids at least fifty percent of the time and did not need to pay child support. He even said since Cherie had never really worked and had spent most of her marital years where she still was—in school, she had not proven that she had in anyway contributed to the family finances. He advised her to graduate and/or get a job. Cherie was furious, but she eventually gave up. She had no money to keep paying for an attorney. Here she was now, in a two bedroom, cracker box of an apartment, working part time in a department store. This is why she had to go to a Kwik Kash just to have money for Christmas. Her whole life had been unfair and unjust and she did not anticipate it getting better.

Walking out of the Kwik Kash, she had relived her whole life in a twinkling of an eye. Yes, she left with $75, but she was still a victim because of other people.

Awaiting announcement of his own future and having his own life flash before his eyes, David suddenly wondered whatever happened to this lady.

CHAPTER ELEVEN

The Survivor

After leaving the Kwik Kash, David and his mom went to the mall to do some Christmas shopping. He smiled smugly to himself wondering how that lady would react if she knew they got $575 instead of just $75. David was not thrilled about another stop, but knew this was his mother's way of trying to make up for all the time she did not spend with him. He figured he could at least get some money from her and buy gifts for Nelson and Daniella. He hoped mom would give him enough to get special gifts, but he doubted it. Scowling, he wondered if he could possibly just "pick up something" without being noticed. He figured if he could get something with the money his mom gave him and show it to her, then no one would suspect him of picking up lingerie or jewelry or another gift that would be super cool to give Daniella. About that time, David noticed something that may just be what he needed-there was a dark grey, brand new Mercedes Benz parked right next to where his mother parked. Inside were gifts almost piled to the roof of the car. There bound to be a gift in there befitting of Daniella. All he needed was the opportunity to get back to the car without mom and before the owner came.

By this tender, yet oddly mature age fourteen, David already knew how to break into cars. He, in fact, had just what he needed in the back of his mom's car, unbeknownst to her, to quickly slip the lock on this car. An older guy for whom he had run some drugs, had given it to him. His problem was getting his mother out of the way so he could get it. As they were entering the Mall, David told his mom he just remembered a jacket he had left in her trunk that would be so cool to wear with his jeans and Nike shoes. His mother protested, but David did the teen sulking, begging, wailing thing and she finally agreed. She gave David the key and told him exactly where to meet her. In fact, she held out giving him spending money to insure he would follow her instructions.

As soon as mom was out of sight, David opened the trunk, wisely took out and put on the jacket and then quickly attempted to break into the car. David was not quite as adept at breaking and entering as he thought. He actually did some damage to the lock, but his primary concern was getting in and getting out before getting caught. He grabbed as many of the packages he could get, especially the small ones. He thought the small ones most likely had jewelry in them. He then went back to his mom's car; pulled up the cover on the jack and spare tire and stored the gifts there. Afterwards, whistling, he sauntered to the agreed upon meeting place with his mom.

As David was entering the Mall, he held the door open for the lady whose arms were full of packages. Michelle was grateful to the pleasant young man and as she walked towards her Mercedes, her mind was preoccupied for what to cook for dinner. As she put her key in the lock, the key refused to slide in as usual. She, thus, shifted her packages and this is when she noticed it—the lock had been damaged and some of her gifts were missing from the car.

The first thoughts Michelle had were she would not let her kids have a Christmas like she used to have. As she mentally stamped her feet and shook her head, the tears gushed from her eyes and her heart felt as if it had a stake driven through it as she recalled what her Christmases had been. Michelle was surprised to find her breathing was shallow and her hands shaking as she began to relive her childhood Christmases.

(Michelle)

Every Christmas, as did most children Michelle would get really excited about Santa Claus. Each year, she would have a somewhat deflated feeling after Christmas arrived, but being younger than six at the time, she never knew why. She became very aware and recognizant of why the Christmas of 1965. By then, she was six years old. That was the Christmas she learned not only was there not a Santa Claus, but why her toys never had that fresh paint look or that spanking brand new feel. She, also, learned why it was never what she actually asked for, for Christmas. That was the year Michelle learned that all of her Christmas (what little bit it was) came from second hand stores and junkyards. Second hand stores might not have been so bad, but junk yard items??? That was more than she could bear even in her recollections. Her dad would actually go to dumps to retrieve Christmas gifts for her. Though this was heartrending, it also was the catalyst to get her where she was today—this was the beginning of the reason she could afford to drive a Mercedes.

Michelle suddenly became "little Michelle" as she was transported back in time by her emotions and her thoughts. As an adult, Michelle knew it was not lack of caring on her father's part, but the pain from childhood was so deep, it was often difficult to truly comprehend this. Michelle felt the penetrating heat of the pain of being so ashamed of her life and her father. Her father was a large hulking, simple man. He didn't have a high school education and he never knew what it was to have material goods. Michelle grew up in the same two-bedroom cottage in which her father had grown up. They did not even have indoor plumbing until she was in high school. Even now standing in the parking lot, she could feel the icy fingers of the cold as she did as a child when she would use the outhouse in the winter. Michelle never invited anyone home with her after she reached the age of six. She had few friends for she was so fearful others would learn of how poverty stricken her family was.

If love had warmed the house, Michelle may have coped better, but she did not even have that warmth to ease the pain of lack of finances. Her father most likely loved her, but just as he did not have the ability to provide all his family needed, he also did not know how to show his love. Michelle remembered how she often would run to him and grab his hand when he would come in from work, but he never squeezed her hand back nor gave her the hugs she craved. She never heard her father say he loved her or was proud of her. Michelle never knew how her father's heart would swell with pride when he looked at her nor how he would feel his bones melt with love when she touched his hand. He did not know how to show affection to her nor did he know he needed to do this. He had grown up so poor himself, all he learned was to be quiet and work hard to at least try to keep the family from starving. Everything outside of food and shelter were alien concepts to him. Michelle's father never knew how it devastated her to not have new, nice Christmas gifts. If he had have known this, he would have died from a broken heart for he had no desire to hurt his little Michelle.

Humiliation, embarrassment and pain the only emotions Michelle knew all of her school years. Going to school did two things for her; it made her aware of how much her family did not have and it motivated her to make sure she never lived that way as an adult. Michelle worked extra hard in school and was a straight A student. She researched grants and scholarships in the school library to insure she was able to go to college and get out of the dump in which she lived. Because of embarrassment of her home life and the driving ambition to "make it", Michelle had very little social life. Her classmates described her as very shy, withdrawn and maybe even a little arrogant. No one knew the suffering Michelle went through every day of her life. Much to her delight, however, she was able to keep her grades up and qualify for college scholarships.

Though she was socially outcast by her own behavior, she still had normal adolescent hormones and she craved love. She, in fact, probably craved love more than the average teen because she did not feel it at home. In her junior year of high school, Michelle met a guy. He was not turned off by her withdrawn quiet nature and would initiate contact with her in the hallways. It got to the place he would walk her to classes and meet her before and after school. Greg never questioned her not inviting him to her home and seemed contented for her to "just meet him" places when they would go out. Michelle began to feel love for and from him and thus, in her mind, included him in her future. Because she thought he felt the same about her as she felt about him, she became sexually intimate with him. The two became a couple and this was the one area in which Michelle was contented. The relationship lasted throughout her junior and senior years of high school. Greg was a year older than Michelle, however, so he graduated a year before she did. He had moved to Tennessee from Arkansas when Michelle was still a senior in high school. He, nevertheless, would write her and when he would come home, they would go out as usual. Michelle, thus, had no reason to think their relationship had changed. Approximately two months before high school graduation, Michelle found she was pregnant. This sort of deviated her from her plans to immediately enter college, but when she broke the news to Greg, be simply suggested she move to Tennessee after graduation. Michelle was elated. Not only would she escape her home life, she would be with a guy who loved her and she would still be able enroll in college after the baby was born. She again researched college grants and scholarships she had to make sure she would be able to use them in Tennessee.

Michelle's classmates noted she seemed much happier towards the end of school, but no one really questioned it nor did they try to form late friendships with her. When school was out, Michelle informed her parents she was moving to Tennessee with Greg. Her father was somewhat gruff in asking if she was sure and her mother was tearful, but glad Michelle was escaping her roots. Michelle was so excited and hopeful as she boarded the bus for Tennessee. She had already written Greg to let him know when she would be there so he could meet her at the bus depot.

Mrs. Richards, Michelle's mom, knew most people would criticize her for letting her eighteen year old go off to live with a guy. Mrs. Richards, though a woman of few words, was a very wise woman. She was well aware of the humiliation Michelle had suffered through the years. She knew it was hard on her to be a part of a family who had as little as they. That was why she never complained when Michelle would not bring Greg home. From pictures and the few things Michelle said about Greg, however, she believed he was a fine young man. He, at least, had been consistent in spending time with Michelle for the past two years.

Though Michelle probably could not yet comprehend this, Mrs. Richards knew that her father loved her very much. He was full of emotional pride when Michelle went to work after school at the local Dairy Freeze. He would almost burst with pride when she brought home her report cards with the A's and when she would make her own clothes that looked store bought. Mr. Richards just did not know how to express this and Mrs. Richards did not know how to explain it to Michelle. She, thus, remained mute and kept all of this within her heart. Michelle was now grown and moving out. Mrs. Richards prayed she was making the right move, would accomplish her goal of college and that she would be happy with Greg. She was just sorry she could not give her something to help her in her new life. She was also regretful that Michelle never mentioned to her about her pregnancy. She knew Michelle did not want to disappoint her and her father and that's why she did not say anything, but a mother knows these things about her daughter. Mrs. Richards bit her tongue as usual and decided to abide her time until her daughter saw fit to share this news. She would by no means make her daughter feel shame about this, but would be waiting to embrace her when she did choose to tell her.

The ride had been long and arduous, but at long last, Michelle arrived in Tennessee. She was so excited to begin her new life with Greg. He had not said they would marry, but she was sure that was the plan since he told her to come. Michelle gathered her meager bags and looked around for Greg. She had told him the e.t.a.; she was sure he must be around somewhere. After watching and waiting for over an hour, Michelle decided to take a taxi to Greg's address. He must have had a late class or worked late or something. She would surprise him by showing up on the doorstep.

Excitedly, Michelle rang Greg's doorbell, but there was no response. On impulse, she tried the doorknob; she was not sure if the crime rate was high here so maybe the door would be unlocked. Heart pounding and smile spreading across her face, she tiptoed inside. She had a brief thought of why he did not meet her since he was obviously here, but she quickly swept this to the back of her mind. Michelle looked around to get her bearings and then headed for a room where she heard noise and sensed movement. As she was preparing to shout "surprise", Michelle saw a woman sitting in Greg's lap, with her hand caressing his hair in a very familiar manner. She dropped her bags and stared before a soft "oh" escaped her lips. Greg looked up, literally dropped the woman and said "Michelle, what are you doing here?" He acted as if she was an acquaintance dropping by and not as if he had expected her.

Feeling dizzy and faint, Michelle backed out of the room and fell into an overstuffed chair behind her. That was when she noticed the feminine touches in the apartment. There were ruffly curtains, female shoes on the floor and framed art that appeared to have been purchased by a woman. Michelle also noticed the color scheme of peaches, cream and green. Could her Greg be living with another woman—the woman in the other room? Greg walked out and attempted to embrace Michelle. Again, she backed away and just stared. Greg's female companion walked into the room and inquired about Michelle.

The conversation thereafter was forever muddled in Michelle's mind. All she held onto was what she learned: Greg was living with this other woman. In fact, this woman was pregnant too. She actually was a month further along than Michelle. When Greg had invited Michelle up, he, apparently, had not believed she would come. He knew she wanted to go to college and had mistakenly assumed she would "come to her senses and abort the baby". He had been involved with this other woman for over a year and had no intention of breaking up with her. Michelle had been his high school plaything and he was moving on with his life. Michelle, in somewhat of a daze, left the apartment, found a cheap motel and passed out for the night. She did not know what her next step was, but she was too tired to even try to figure it out right then.

Awaking the next morning, Michelle still fully clothed, felt disoriented, out of sorts and slightly gripped with an unknown fear. Shaking her head, she suddenly remembered the night previously. Tears slowly ran down her face as Michelle looked into a bleak future. She could not go back home, a failure. This threw a major wrench in her plans. Primarily, being a practical person, Michelle decided first things first. She slowly got up, took a long hot shower in the tiny motel bathroom, dressed and then sat to count what money she had left from her part time job. Michelle decided her next plan of action was to find a job here, a small apartment and an obstetrician. Once these things were in place, then she would have to call her mother.

Even now standing in the parking lot, Michelle remembered the cold rationale and calm that had overtaken her. She had decided to take charge of her life and not be a victim. Michelle had called her mom who was not only not shocked by the pregnancy, but instead, was very supportive of Michelle's future plans. Michelle had found a job at a nearby diner, found a tiny efficiency apartment and decided to enroll in a couple of classes at a junior college. Once again, Michelle was playing many roles, but this determination is what actually saved her.

Six and one half months after that nightmare day at Greg's place, Michelle gave birth to a healthy eight pound baby girl. Michelle never knew it was possible to feel so much love, responsibility and fear all at once. She, however, would make a life for her and her little girl. The baby was born right after spring break so this gave Michelle enough time to enroll at the local university for the Fall Semester. She had saved enough money from her job to have her mother come and spend a couple of weeks with her after the baby was born. Her boss, who had a crush on her, gave her maternity leave with pay. Michelle was on her way.

The arrival of the Fall Semester brought other changes that Michelle initially viewed as good. Her baby was enrolled in the University child-care nursery and Michelle met a handsome, intelligent, six-foot colleague with skin the color of butterscotch. He, like Michelle, was a pre-med student. When Brad saw the voluptuous, cinnamon brown skinned, dark eyed, five foot six, serious minded looking woman his first day of class, he knew this was the woman for him. He was immediately drawn to her and manipulated his way into her line of vision. He pretended to want to make sure he was in the right class, but he really just wanted to hear her voice. When she spoke in that cultured, yet honey toned voice, Brad knew he was a goner.

Michelle had already noticed Brad before he eased his way over to her. She was flattered he noticed her, but immediately experienced anxiety. She could not be distracted from her studies; had remember she was a mother and stay focused on her goals. Brad, however, won her over shortly after their initial meeting. He did not seem to have a problem with her being a single mom and he too indicated being focused on his own career track.

After two years of dating and studying together, Brad and Michelle married. What she had not known during their courtship was that Brad had one major flaw—a gambling habit. She knew he was often short of money, but this was typical for students. This was why the couple, along with the baby, had moved into Family Student Housing. Michelle had figured this was a way for them to save money and still be able to provide for their needs. She never wanted to live as she had in her parents' home and she did not want her daughter to live this way ever.

Within a year of marriage, Michelle realized the lack of money was not always due to the lack of income. With her scholarships, Brad's scholarships, their part time jobs and Elizabeth being able to stay at the campus nursery, the family should not have been struggling the way they sometimes did. Soon thereafter, Brad's moods began to swing, his grades dropped and he was often gone without Michelle having any idea where he was. He began to act grumpy when she would inquire and their marriage slowly disintegrated. When the phone calls began coming in the middle of the night and Brad insisted he answer all calls as well as always get the mail, Michelle became very suspicious. One day, Michelle noticed an official looking piece of mail from the university business and admissions office. Against her better judgment, but listening to her intuition, she opened it. That was when she learned Brad had been put on probation and then actually asked to leave school. It seems he was heavily in debt from gambling; had taken school loans and grants, but had not been attending classes nor was he able to account for the money. He, in fact, had registered for classes, but had gradually withdrawn from several classes in order to partial refund of tuition. Michelle was once again devastated and hurt by someone for whom she had given her love and trust. She dreaded the confrontation but knew she would have to talk with Brad. Reaching her goals and providing for her daughter were the most important priorities in her life; thus, what had to be done had to be done.

With a lump the size of the tennis ball in her throat and tears which felt like golf balls running down her face, Michelle confronted Brad when he got home. Initially, he responded with anger and denial, blaming the school for the computer screwing up things. He insisted he would go tomorrow and 'straighten this out'. Michelle, nevertheless, knew within her heart that the letter was valid. She told Brad there was nothing to straighten out, but his life. Brad broke down in tears, begged Michelle's forgiveness, said he would go to gambler's anonymous and repay all of the debt. Michelle wanted so badly to believe him, she agreed. Brad did exactly what he promised for about three months, but then the same cycle began and this time she received a letter from the business office, stating they would have to begin garnishing her work study checks and her scholarships. This was the last straw, so with broken heart and spirit, Michelle divorced Brad and tried once again to begin her life anew.

For the next two years, Michelle concentrated only on her studies and her daughter, Elizabeth. By now Elizabeth was a fairly cheerful, sociable child. Having started her life in daycare facilities, albeit learning facilities for college students, she showed no fear of others. Elizabeth, unlike Michelle had been, would initiate with others and was welcomed others into her life. Though this was a foreign concept for Michelle, she took pleasure in her daughter taking pleasure from life. In addition, it helped her out that Elizabeth had playmates and she had no qualms about having some of her playmate's parents baby-sit Elizabeth. This simply allowed Michelle to work part time and accelerate her studies. She had now completed her undergraduate work, was working as a dental assistant intern and Elizabeth was happily anticipating entering kindergarten in a few months.

Unlike high school, Michelle actually had a few friends. Since she no longer lived as poverty stricken and most of her friends were college students, as well, she did not feel isolated. Michelle felt no shame of her life, but rather, felt pride in what she was accomplishing. She would feel some guilt and anger when she thought of the fact that Elizabeth did not know and would never know her biological father. Greg had never tried to contact Michelle since the day she walked out of his apartment. He dropped off the face of the earth as far as Michelle was concerned. Michelle had been so pleased with Brad's relationship with Elizabeth and had hoped he and she would one day give her a sibling. He, too, was gone now; he, unlike Greg, had often tried to contact her and get back with her after their divorce, but Michelle could not risk the problems of living with a compulsive gambler. She could not and would not live that way nor allow her baby to suffer that humiliation. Here she and Elizabeth were—alone once again.

One late, endless Friday night when Elizabeth was staying overnight with a friend, Michelle felt the familiar sharp pain of loneliness. She missed Brad so much and she wanted someone in her life. She, however, was too fearful to even go out with the guys who did flirt with her and ask her out. She did not have the privileged option of dating casually—she had goals and a child. If she was to get involved, it had to be serious, leading to permanency. Michelle, nevertheless, was uncomfortable with this, too; look where her other two serious relationships landed her! At age twenty-four, Michelle needed a normal life—one had never had. She was extremely lonely and lonesome, so when she noticed the television ad about a dating service, she actually took down the information. She berated herself for even considering this, for this could only lead to danger, heartache and more temporary situations in her life. Michelle called one of her fellow students and casually mentioned the ad. Her friend was delighted Michelle would even think about it. She had tried, in vain, for months to get Michelle to go out. Maybe, this was the opportunity so she strongly encouraged her. Michelle began hesitating and thinking rationally. Her friend told her she was on the way; her husband and children were already asleep and she and Michelle lived down the sidewalk from each other. She came right over and almost forced Michelle to follow through on information. By one a.m., Michelle found herself one of the newest members of a dating on line service. Was she crazy? Most likely, but maybe it would be a fun diversion from all of heavy life responsibilities.

After Michelle's friend left, Michelle went to bed, feeling more peaceful and relaxed than she had in years. The next morning, actually waking afresh, she remembered what she had done the night previously. What had she been thinking? She, however, figured nothing would come of it and she would chalk it up to a night of fatigue and poor impulses. As the day wore on, Elizabeth called and begged her to let her stay one more night at her friend's. After clearing this with the parents, Michelle, grudgingly relented. This left her again with that void and depression she had felt the previous night. Michelle realized her life was so enmeshed in Elizabeth, school and work, that when she had any free time, she had no idea what to do with it. She paced, picked up and put down her schoolbooks, made herself a light breakfast, flipped through some magazines and channel surfed. Michelle felt so antsy and disturbed; she finally gave in and dialed the television on-line dating service. Much to her surprise, when she called the number and entered her code, there were several messages waiting for her. This peaked her curiosity and she had a whole day of freedom so she decided to listen.

As Michelle listened to the different male voices, she found herself, intrigued, amused, and in some cases, scared. The one voice that really attracted her, however, was the deep voiced, African American male that identified himself as Alvin Greene. Though he did not say anything different from the others, Michelle still found herself irresistibly drawn to and excited by that voice. Michelle decided since she had come with far, she might as well respond to some of the messages to "see what would happen". In her heart of hearts, however, her only desire was to hear from Alvin. The very practical minded Michelle did respond to several of the messages and had some surprisingly pleasant conversations. She set several blind dates with a variety of men of diverse ethnic, economic and social backgrounds. She did not immediately hear from Alvin, but left him a message in his voice mailbox. Astonishingly, Michelle found that dating in reality enhanced her life instead of imposing on or interfering with it. Even Elizabeth seemed happier and Michelle enjoyed her time with Elizabeth more now that this was not the only composition of her social life.

Several days passed before Michelle heard from Alvin. Michelle had essentially put her desire to meet/ hear from him in the recesses of her mind. Her heart, nonetheless, would beat a little quicker each time she checked her box and learned she had new messages. At last, she heard the deep, alluring voice of Alvin. She was amazed at her reaction to a voice. Breathlessly, she returned his call and heard him speaking with her. The two connected so well, each often forgot they had not met in person. They spoke for several weeks via phone because Alvin insisted he was "the one" for Michelle so he preferred her to get the rest of "those morons" out of her system before they met. He told her she would be tied to him for life once they met, so enjoy her time now. Michelle would giggle softly at this, knowing how ludicrous this was. At the same time, though, there was something about this flirtatious statement that sounded prophetic. It was nothing she could explain or rationalize, but it was a veritable conviction within her very being.

Michelle talked to her neighbor and friend about all of her dates and phone calls; yet, there was a notable difference in her tone when she spoke of Alvin. In addition, she shared less of the details of her conversations with Alvin with her friend. When this was pointed out to her, she vehemently denied it, but in the quiet moments, she became terrifyingly aware how much veracity was in this accusation. Michelle found herself musing over what their first date would encompass and if she would be disappointed in him when she saw him in person. Over the phone, he seemed to suit her so well. Michelle had met and liked several of the guys with whom she went out, but couldn't shake her interest in and anticipation of meeting Alvin. In moments of rationale, Michelle would take stock of what she was doing and hope she was not missing out on some potentially good relationships because of her obsession with Alvin. This never stopped the rat a tat, tat of her heart each time she thought of him and heard his voice.

The day of the date with Alvin arrived. Michelle had barely been able to concentrate or focus on her work and studies all day. About two hours before time to meet, the phone rang. Michelle's heart froze when she heard Alvin's voice. She felt so despondent, knowing he had to be calling to cancel their date. He hem hawed around and said he needed to tell her something. Michelle just knew she would pass out from the disappointment and hurt. What Alvin said next totally blew her mind—it was so unlike her expectation. All he wanted to tell her before they met was his name was not really Alvin. Though later Michelle pondered this eschewed truth, at that moment, she felt nothing except relief. He was not standing her up. His last name was Greene, but his first name was really Joshua. When asked why he had pretended his name was Alvin, he said he thought no one would believe an African American would really be named Joshua. Alvin, or rather Joshua, said he wanted to come clean with her because he already felt deep feelings for Michelle. They, then, confirmed where and when they would meet that night.

Michelle had learned that Alvin/Joshua loved Chinese food and so did she, so she had picked out a restaurant that she often frequented. Alvin lived about forty-five minutes away so though he knew how to get to her small town, he did not know a lot about it. They agreed to meet at a convenience market right off the interstate exit. Michelle arrived early and sat, trying to slow her fast beating heart, and vainly, tried to keep her sweaty palms dry. She turned on her favorite music station while waiting though as distracted as she was, she heard none of the songs. Her mind was too focused on "what ifs". What if he did not show? What if he did not like her? What if she did not like him? What if he turned out to be the exact opposite of what he was on the phone? What if he had a wreck? What if he was criminal, a rapist, a scam artist? What if she liked him and he could not stand her? And so on and so on and so on. What seemed like hours later, but really was only seven minutes later, she saw his car drive up. He parked right next to her, shook his head a little when he saw her and then burst into a smile. The two exited their respective cars and it was instantaneous recognition. It was as if they knew each other's souls and spirits. They began laughing, hugged and spoke. Joshua seemed so familiar to Michelle, she decided to ride with him to the restaurant instead of having him follow her. As a general rule, Michelle had all of her blind dates meet her in neutral spots and then go to chosen destination in their own cars.

The ride was not as awkward as would have been anticipated and the couple immediately engaged in teasing banter. Michelle spent most of the ride and dinner, teasingly calling Alvin, Alvin Joshua. After two hours, the couple did not want to leave each other's company so they rode around town, talking even more. As it was later learned, both were actually reserved, introverted, private people. As they learned this in later months about each other, this first meeting seemed even more amazing and maybe, even predestined.

As the evening drew to an end, Michelle's only thought was that she fervently wished Joshua would call her again as he said he would. Michelle reminisced about the evening and recalled how very attractive Joshua was. She had dated several attractive men; had been married to a very handsome guy and had a daughter by a good-looking man. None of them, however, compared to Joshua for he was exceptionally attractive both inside and outside. He was sweet, kind and had a great sense of humor. He was about 5'10", 185 pounds, and had skin the color of brown sugar. He wore his hair closely shaved and he had a neatly trimmed moustache and goatee. Even thinking of him stirred emotions deep within Michelle's heart and soul. She attempted to not get her hopes up that there would be a relationship with the two of them, but that stirring of hope surfaced and resurfaced several times throughout the night.

Not only did Joshua call the next day, but also, he called again and again and again. For the first time in Michelle's life, she had someone in her life that she loved, whom she felt loved her and whom she felt healthy love with her daughter. As Michelle stood in that parking lot, she gave most of the credit of her life taking a positive turn to Joshua. He had stayed with her, encouraged her while she was in medical school, supported her starting her own dental business and in the midst of all of that, he married her. Joshua did not have any negative habits that would affect them detrimentally and he remained consistent to this day.

Michelle looked at her slightly damaged car, noted some of the gifts were missing, but then took a deep breath and smiled. She was not that lonely, poor little girl anymore. She was not a betrayed pregnant girlfriend. She was not a hurt wife with a husband with a gambling problem. Michelle was a successful dentist with her own practice; a husband who loved her; a husband who not only adopted her daughter, but was the father of her son. No matter how many gifts were missing, they could be replaced. In addition, nothing was taking away their lovely house and loving home, Michelle went around to the passenger side of her car; crawled in and drove home, smiling all the way. Michelle was no longer a victim—Michelle was a survivor!!

(David)

After entering the Mall, David never saw Michelle again. He never knew she was the one whose car he had robbed. Sitting in juvenile, he wondered why he had even thought of her. Though he was recalling some of the mistakes he had made, including burglarizing that Mercedes, he did not know what the connection was between this and his remembering the lady at the Mall.

Ironically, David was able to hide all of the gifts he had taken from the car, but none of them were appropriate for Daniella. The gifts held savings bonds, key rings, some old pin he had heard someone call a broach and various and sundry other items that were not appealing to David. He could not believe he had wasted his time breaking into such a nice car for such sorry gifts.

CHAPTER TWELVE

The Bulimic/Lesbian

Despite the fact that David had not 'scored' with the Mercedes, he had managed to buy Daniella some really cool earrings, as well as an ankle bracelet. He was looking forward to giving them to her and tonight was the night. He, Nelson and Daniella had been invited as guests of Summer's to attend a Christmas party. Daniella suggested they not wait until Christmas, but should exchange gifts at the party.

Nelson was so excited when he got to David's. He had gifts for all of his friends, including Summer. He showed the I.D. bracelet to David that his grandmother had bought for him to give Summer. David expressed approval and showed Nelson his gifts for Daniella. He and Nelson had bought each other CD's. They then left for Daniella's; David's mom drove them there. Summer would meet them there and they would ride over to the party in Daniella's car.

When they arrived at Daniella's, they barely heard Mrs. O'Brien's instructions on how to behave, when to be home, etc., they were so excited. Daniella was wearing a glittering off the shoulder mini dress while Summer wore a jade green, festive jumpsuit. They both looked so good, David and Nelson almost forgot they had gifts. As the gifts were dropping out of their hands, they were brought back to reality; spoke and exchanged gifts. Both Summer Daniella had bought them matching leather wallets with their initials engraved. The girls loved their gifts and Summer was touched that Nelson had been so thrilled at his gift for her. She realized how deep his crush was and that is why she had given him the wallet. She would never hurt him by laughing at him. Besides, she felt safe with him for she knew he was not emotionally mature enough to pursue her like a normal teen-aged boy and presently that was fine with her. Summer then told them they were going to the Christmas party at the Lawrence home.

David and Nelson stared in awe when they arrived at the Lawrence home. It was as large if not larger than Daniella's. Daniella did not know the Lawrences either, but being used to this kind of lifestyle, she was not as awestruck. When they walked in the foyer, David thought this area was so large, his parents' garage would fit inside here. As he and Nelson stared wide eyed, this luscious looking, auburn haired, grey eyed female walked forward and extended a hand of welcome. Summer introduced her as Mrs. Devora Lawrence—this was Summer's friend's mother! She spoke with a cultured voice; she was so nice. About that time, a young girl with a man following close behind, entered the foyer. This was Dawn. Dawn had her blonde hair cut into a stylish page boy; wore long dangling earrings, short black leather skirt and a loose red Christmas sweater. With her light brown eyes and shy grin, Dawn introduced her father, Mr. Brent Lawrence. Mr. Lawrence had a large muscular build and dark olive skin. During this brief introduction, the friends learned Dawn was a sixteen-year old high school student, her mother was an officer in the military and her father was a carpenter. Her parents told them they were happy to meet them; the rest of the guests were in the basement and admonished Dawn that they would be upstairs out of the way, but available for anything the young people needed. This was the life.

The party was great. The music was happening and all of the kids were nice. Dawn was a very nice girl, although David sensed she was 'hiding something'. Since he himself usually had something on back burner, he was more aware of this tension than the others were. He mentioned it to Daniella and Summer, but they both insisted she was just shy. Nevertheless, after that night, Dawn was often a regular with the group. David, thus, learned a lot about Dawn; he, however, did not ever learn of the deep dark secrets the family harbored. He believed, as did most of the world, that here was one more family who had it all.

Behind closed doors of the Lawrence house there was pain, frustration and humiliation. Mr. & Mrs. Lawrence met as upward mobile twenty somethings.

Devora had entered the military when she was eighteen and had completed a college degree there. When seeking to build her own home, she had met her then spouse to be, Brent. Brent was a carpenter and had been contracted out to build the kitchen and bathroom cabinets. When Devora met Brent, she felt immediate comfort with him and he felt immediate infatuation tor her. Devora was attracted to Brent because he was shy, yet friendly; not handsome, but fairly attractive in a gentle looking way. This was in such contrast to his profession of carpentry. Devora, on the other hand, was obviously self-confident, cultured, and was attractive in a wholesome way. She was not a beauty queen; yet, she had a smoldering sexuality about her that both the young and old male population found almost irresistible. Furthermore, though men fell at her feet, she treated them with almost total disregard. She never seemed effected by their adoration and those guys with whom she was a friend, felt honored.

Devora and Brent fell into an easy friendship that eventually led to a comfortable relationship. They found they could talk to each other without fear or vulnerability risks. Each trusted the other implicitly and so after two years of comradeship when Brent proposed, Devora accepted. Brent had often wondered if something was missing from the courtship in that Devora was often secretive about her whereabouts; he, nevertheless, contributed this to her job—she was a very critical wheel in her profession. Not only did this tug at the edges of his mind occasionally, he also noted how she seemed to never be concerned about his whereabouts or show any interest in his female relationships, past or present. He determined to not look a gift horse in the mouth, but instead to appreciate a woman showing complete faith and trust in him. Pushing all doubts to the side, Brent proposed. Devora accepted and the couple married. They moved into the home Devora had, had built and which Brent had helped build. All appeared perfect.

The marriage was fairly uneventful. Devora traveled a lot with her job and Brent stayed busy assisting building contractors as well as doing side jobs of renovation for his own personal customers. After about three years of marriage, Brent realized he and Devora had never discussed having children. He really wanted children and had assumed Devora would, too. Since she was quickly approaching her late twenties/early thirties, Brent decided to broach the subject. He was completely taken off guard when Devora stated she did not want children. He was dumbfounded; how could this wonderful woman not want children? Devora said she thought Brent knew she was not maternal and was more career-oriented. This actually put a slight wrench in their intimate life for a brief time. It was only slight because the couple was not the most physically interactive couple anyway. Brent always attributed this to Devora being so busy.

Eventually, Brent chose to push the issue of having children for he loved children and really wanted to experience fatherhood. Though Devora was surprised at this uncharacteristic assertiveness, she was pleased with this show of manhood, so she acquiesced to attempt to become pregnant at least once. After about six months, she did indeed become pregnant. Brent was thrilled about the child; he was even more thrilled at how soft and feminine

Devora was during pregnancy. He had not realized what a masculine edge she had about her before because she was so physically feminine looking. As he pondered her behaviors, it became very clear how she tended to be very aggressive, controlling and domineering most of the time. She showed no interest in stereotyped feminine matters and was her happiest when working. Seeing her this feminine and soft, thus, came as a welcome shock. During her pregnancy, Devora was gentler, less aggressive and less abrasive. It served only to make Brent love her even more. Despite the lack of excitement and intense passion Brent desired for his marriage, he still very much loved his wife. He received more of the love and attention he desired of her during her pregnancy than at any other time of their marriage. He fervently hoped this behavior/attitude would continue postpartum.

With the exception of the attitude change, Devora's pregnancy was uneventful. When she came full term, the healthy baby girl was named Dawn. When Brent looked at her, he could not believe the overwhelming emotions of love, fear, protection, fulfillment, etc., he experienced. This was what life was meant to be. This had to be his mission in life. He looked at that seven-pound bundle of life that no one but he and Devora could have created. Brent had never felt such pride or more manly in his life. He was astonished at how Devora only smiled at the baby and then made plans to immediately return to work. He was so sure she would want to stay home with the baby, at least for a few months. He knew she could take the time from work since she had rank and there was no impending war. Brent figured she was just tired from giving birth and once they were home, he was sure Devora would fall as much in love with Dawn as he had instantaneously done.

Once the little family arrived home and settled into a routine, Brent quickly found himself the caregiver of Dawn. He loved being her dad, but felt Devora should have more input and concern. Devora primarily concerned that the baby had the "right" clothes, food, proper baby material things and that she was developing as quickly or quicker as other children her age. Other than this, she spent very little time with the child. She had even suggested his mom could spend time and take care of the baby so she could go on back to work. She seldom cuddled or rocked her unless the purpose was to put her to sleep so she (Devora) could attend to her own personal needs. Not only did Devora lose the soft femininity she had during pregnancy, she resumed working harder than ever; spent more time away from home and their intimate life became practically nonexistent. Brent convinced himself this was a short term, postpartum situation. Five years later, as things had not progressed, he became resigned to this way of life. He was not happy, but he had his baby Dawn, around whom he thought the galaxies centered. This was his joy in life and so he determined his lot in life was to be a dad and a carpenter.

As Dawn got older and Devora still gave her no special attention nor was she attentive to Bret's needs, he began questioning what was happening. She would dismiss his inquiries with mumbled replies and no true responses. Brent took this for a while, but when Dawn began questioning why mom was never around and she did not seem to care to be with the family, he pushed the issue with Devora. This only led to verbal battle and to Devora completely pushing Brent away. Not only was she not interested in physical intimacy with Brent, she insisted they have separate bedrooms. She no longer included Brent in her activities, either social or professionally.

By the time Dawn turned twelve, she was well aware that her parents were not a real couple. She, in fact, became withdrawn and secretive. Her parents contributed this to the onset of adolescence. In reality, Dawn felt so out of control of her life and wanted so badly to be "normal" as other teens. She worked daily to appear happy, go lucky and she tried to keep her home life a secret from her peers. Ironically, though mom paid little attention to their family, she continued to engage in "the right things" so for every stage of life, Devora insisted on doing things for Dawn. She insisted on taking her and her friends to shop for brand name clothes. She insisted on the occasional weekend teen social at the house. By then, she had insured that Brent had built them a bigger home so she actually had rooms set aside just for Dawn and her friends. She tried to force Dawn into what she considered normal teen behavior, which only served to stress Dawn more. This is when it began for Dawn—the eating and purging cycle. She would get such a high and feel this was the one time she was in full control of everything that happened to her and her body. Ironically, Dawn did not feel the need to control what she looked like as much as the fact that no matter how her mother complained, she could not force Dawn to not binge and purge. The first time she discovered this activity was actually coincidental. There had been another cycle of silent treatment, scream and yell, ignore everything and everybody in her home. At dinnertime, it was the time for ignoring everyone so she had to get her own meal and was sitting in silence eating her potpie. Looking around at her beautiful surroundings and feeling the coldness of living there, literally made Dawn sick to her stomach. She, however, felt such a release from vomiting, she felt high. She suddenly felt renewed and desired to eat something sweet. She had raided the kitchen cabinets and eaten everything in sight that required minimal or no preparation. When she became overly full, she did not wait for the discomfort of the sick feeling, but instead forced vomiting. Again, that high feeling of release and being in control occurred. Dawn did not immediately begin this cycle routinely, but would only binge and purge when feeling her most stressed and out of control. Then the day came when she began doing this everyday because she found out just what a roller coaster she really was riding and advertising it as life.

Brent suspected Devora was having an affair. She spent even less time at home, was more withdrawn, if that was possible and Brent could see it was having a detrimental effect on Dawn. He would hear Dawn vomiting in her bathroom often after meals. He did not know what to do. He tentatively approached Devora, who waved him away and later, jumped Dawn to 'stop this foolishness'. This, of course, changed nothing. Brent tried to question Devora about his suspicions about her having a boyfriend. Just as she did with Dawn, Devora suggested he 'cease his foolish talking'. In fact, she told him she had no desire to be with any man. Brent heard her, but he continued to see her dress seductively and leave home for hours at a time. He saw how she continued to ignore Dawn, except when reprimanding her or planning another "teen social" for her, despite Dawn's protests that she did not want these. Brent began to walk as if walking on egg shells, never talked to Devora unless she addressed him first; attempted to maintain a relationship with his daughter and basically suffered in silence—convinced Devora was involved with another man. He knew she spent a lot of time with Stephen. Though he had never noticed any sideward glances or air of intimacy with them, they spent a lot of time together. This, in fact, was one of the few friends Devora allowed in her home. She did not try to hide the relationship; would talk to him on the phone and would not hesitate to tell Dawn she was running over to Stephen's. Brent was convinced this was the guy and that they were being very obvious so it would cover the fact of the reality of it.

They day Dawn jumped on the almost endless cycle of purging and bingeing without any daily breaks was the same day she could have told Brent what Devora was doing. The incessant cycle coincided and was fully triggered by her discovery that day.

It was a weekday and Dawn had left school early due to feeling ill. The office had not called her mother, but rather had called her father for permission. They had long learned if they needed to reach one of the Lawrences, it would have to be Mr. Lawrence. Brent, of course, was very concerned, but Dawn had assured him it was just the discomfort of cramps—she'd be fine; just needed to go home and lie down. He gave permission and she drove herself home. Upon arrival, Dawn had planned to park as far over to the side as possible so as to not block her parents' entrance to the garage. To her amazement, her mom's car was already there. This evoked a mixture of dread since she did not know what mood mom would be in and peace since she was ill and would like the comfort of a mom. Dawn parked and ran into the side door. She stopped in her tracks when she heard voices that did not sound as if they were coming from the television. That is when it dawned on her there had been a foreign car in front of the house. She was accustomed to seeing Stephen's car in the drive, but it was not his. The unfamiliar car and the unexpectedness of her mom being home instilled caution into her. She slowed her tracks and actually began tipping towards the voices.

Dawn could tell the voices were coming from the downstairs guest room. She eased toward the door and heard her mother's breathless giggle. Her mother never giggled; she was too formal and cultured. Her mother almost sounded young and carefree. Dawn moved closer and silently pushed open the well-oiled door. Thank God her mom was such a stickler for everything sounding and running smoothly. Dawn felt sick and lightheaded as she realized her dad was probably right—her mom was probably having an affair. He had to be wrong about Stephen though for it was definitely not his car or his voice. Besides, though her dad did not know this, Dawn had long since learned Stephen was gay. If he had a romantic interest in anyone in that house, it would have been her dad.

As Dawn quietly stuck her head around the door, she almost vomited in the hallway at what she had witnessed. Tears flowed down her face and her mind was a swirl of disbelief, hurt, anger and denial. No wonder her mom was always gone; no wonder she was so secretive. No wonder she had no time for her or her dad. Her mom was definitely having an affair. It could not be called anything, but an affair. Her mother was fully nude as well as her bed partner. They were giggling and rolling around on the bed, mussing each other's hair and doing all sorts of things no teen wants to see their parents do; not with each other or any one else. This, believe it or not, was not the most horrible revelation of it all. The revelation that sent Dawn to the bathroom vomiting and vomiting and vomiting until she passed out was she had witnessed her mother being intimate with another woman.

Devora was so engrossed with her lover, she did not know Dawn had seen her. Devora had known for years that she was attracted to women. She had done all she could to not give into this. She had dated many males and had married Brent. She loved Brent in a comfy way; she was not romantically in love with him. She often regretted his suffering, but she could not divorce him. Devora knew this would be the kindest thing to do for Brent, but it would utterly destroy her career. Being an open lesbian in the military would be professional suicide. She had to maintain the façade of her marriage in order to maintain her career.

During the Christmas party for her daughter, Devora had actually been pondering the facts of her marriage and the desire to be with the one she truly loved. Life was really strained with Brent since she had to "act the part" or totally ignore him. The former was not fair to her and the latter was not fair to him. This was one of those nights when it weighed heavily on her mind since both of them needed to be home at the same time for the teen social. As she glanced at her watch, she could tell this was going to be a long night. About that time, the phone rang; it was probably "her". Maybe tonight would not be as long as she had anticipated.

While Devora was happily anticipating possibly meeting her friend for the night, Brent was sitting clothed in his misery in the library. This should be a time when he and Devora were celebrating Christmas, their lives together and the fact that their daughter was getting older. Instead, here they sat, in separate parts of the house, each in his/her own worlds. Furthermore, Brent knew within his heart of hearts that all was not right with Dawn; this vomiting had to be more than teenage behavior. He, however, did not know how to reach her nor did he know how to communicate with Devora. He, thus, simply sat and stared at the book, lined walls.

While the elder Lawrences were wallowing in their own private hells, Dawn was smiling brightly on the outside with her friends. Inwardly, she too was torn. She knew what her mother was really like and she had never confronted her. She wanted to take the pain from the father she loved, but she feared telling him about her mom would only create a more intense pain for him.

She could barely wait for her guests to leave so she could vomit in private.

As David, Nelson, Summer and Danielle were leaving, each was thinking what a great night it had been and how lucky Dawn was. They wished they had parents who would give them parties like this. They had even been allowed to drink a little champagne. The Lawrence family was so cool. Each person was so wrapped in individual thoughts, no one had any idea what private pains the others were experiencing.

CHAPTER THIRTEEN

David

After the party high wore off, David became very somber in his thoughts about Daniella. She seemed to really like his gifts, but he also acknowledged how very comfortable she was at the Lawrence home. Daniella was very used to a higher standard of living than David was. He felt more inadequate than before, that he would never be able to give Daniella the things to which she was accustomed. What if some older, wealthier guy came along and Daniella realized he was just a "poor kid"? David had to find a way to buy the type of gifts he thought Daniella would want. This simply led him to another spree of shoplifting. When Daniella would protest that he gave her too much and inquire how he managed to get money for all of this, David would sidetrack her. He would respond with "how he loved her" and "how she deserved this stuff" and how she need never worry "her pretty little head" over these matters. Daniella was rather offended by the last and suspicious considering she had heard of his reputation, but she always let it drop.

By the age of fifteen, David was full of confidence about his ability to "take what he wanted". He had tried to be legitimate for Daniella, but he needed too many things. It was hard to be a teenager and especially one who was in love. He, thus, continued to "pick up" things as he needed them. Some were little gifts for Daniella, some were foodstuffs as candies, some were CD's, etc… His largest items, however, were some he considered the most necessary—clothing. David needed to dress cool and either he could not afford the clothes or his mom would say he did not need certain things. In addition to this, there was still a certain thrill in being able to get away with stealing.

When David would take brand name sweatshirts, jeans and athletic shoes home, his mom would inquire as to how he attained them. He usually told her he had gotten them from cutting yards for someone or that Daniella had bought it (his mom knew Daniella had money) or some other bogus story. He would say just about anything his mom would believe.

David had noticed that warm, sunny days were the days he tended to get his most bored and restless. It was as if the sun shining, the birds singing, the warmth of the air and the generally good mood of all of the people in the streets mocked David—made him insignificant. He had to be more than the rest of the people and this led him to committing some foolish acts. These days were worst than the dark, dreary, stormy days that at least reflected his inner turmoil.

It was a bright, clear & sunny day the day David met Michael. He was wandering around a large department store, deciding which outfit to shoplift. He had a date with Daniella that night and he wanted a new, brand named outfit. David was generally quite adept at walking out with these clothing. He would do the typical take several items to the dressing room; keep on the ones he wanted underneath his other clothes and then return the rest to the return rack of discarded items. He would then walk around the store some more, often even purchasing some small items, such as gum or mints. Walking out the store with his little purchases in plain sight and his new clothes underneath his, he would be very confident appearing as he left the premises. His heart was usually pounding and his hands sweaty, but this was more from the thrill of it all as opposed to the fear.

Today was no different. David tried on several outfits, chose the one he wanted, discarded the rest and then actually bought a CD this time. He found the bars were often left on the CD's so if the alarm sounded, the store personnel would see his sales ticket, think the CD set off the alarm and let him go. As he was leaving this time, though, a tall, burly chest, red haired, green-eyed Caucasian male continued to yell "hey" at him. Since he was dressed in tan slacks, soft -soled black shoes and black pullover, David stopped. Maybe he wanted David to "work for him". Gentleman of this type, seemed to often stop David to "run little errands" for some money. It generally involved delivering unmarked packages, taking little gifts to women who obviously were not their wives or other such things that David thought might be illegal, but did not care. He just wanted the money and he liked knowing he had knowledge that could be powerful. Since this guy looked like this and he had no indications of working at this store, David eagerly responded. Big mistake!! This was a plains clothed in-store detective. He knew David had the clothes on underneath. David attempted outrage, anger, denial, and then acted as if fearfully sorry. Nothing worked. This guy, called Michael, took him to the back of the store; made him undress; threatened to call his mother and the police, but then for some reason, told David since he could simply return the items right then, he was letting him off with a warning. David thanked him profusely, but inside, he was fuming, his emotions furling and boiling. What would "Michael" know about needing brand name clothing and not having the money? What did he know about being underage so unable to get steady work? He had a job—a powerful, sneaky one in David's mind—and he probably had a nice car, a big house, a pretty wife and two point five children. David was furious, but he actually used judgment and did not let it show. He simply exited the store and made plans to stop at another one and be more careful.

(The Store Detective)

David was right about several things about the thirty-year old Michael. He had a nice car—a new Toyota Camry, a large house—5 BR, 3 BA, 2 car garage in the right neighborhood, a wife of ten years and an eight year old son and six year old daughter. Past those accurate assumptions, however, David could not possibly comprehend Michael's life.

When Michael met Whitney Springfield, he was not initially attracted or impressed. The first turn off was her name—Whitney. What self-respecting parents would name their daughter Whitney? Physically, he was not attracted to her either. Michael liked the standard, 5'8" or taller, model thin, blue-eyed, long straight haired blondes. Whitney was none of this. She barely stood 5'4". Though not overweight, she was not thin—she was more curvaceous with a medium boned frame. Whitney had dark chocolate natural curly hair and tawny colored eyes. He had met her at a club one night and she had approached him. His buddies had ribbed him and encourage him to talk to her, but she was not his type. She continued to talk to him anyway and actually when the night came to an end, he had determined she might not be "that bad". By the time he walked her to her car and discovered she had a new, midnight blue corvette convertible, he had to ashamedly admit, his interest in her grew. Whitney slipped him her phone number, which was on a business card, and drove off into the darkness of the night.

When Michael's friends looked at the card, they high fived each other, slapped him on the back and screamed with disbelief. Michael stared at them as if they had lost their minds and was about to chalk it up to intoxication when one said, "you really don't know, do you?" Michael had responded with "Know what?" That is when he learned Whitney was the only child of the mogul of

Springfield Industries. A company at which everyone wanted to work and the owner of whom owned most of the town in one form or another. Why would Whitney be interested in him? Was this some kind of joke? Again, shamefacedly, Michael had to admit to himself, this made her more attractive. Forget what he said was his type; he never could get that kind of girl anyway! He decided he would definitely call her the following day. The cold, sober daylight should assist him in figuring if this was a relationship worth pursuing.

The next day Michael got up his nerve to call Whitney. Her home, work, pager and cell phone numbers were listed. Michael called her home and she answered immediately. She knew it was him and at that time, he did not know if this was some uncanny premonition or caller ID. Whitney answered with "Hi, there, Michael" and then proceeded to tell him their plans for that night. It was a Saturday and Michael had no plans, but this took him off guard. He, however, liked this because he had difficulty making decisions. It was nice for him to have this "take charge" person making plans. He agreed to meet her at a restaurant he had only passed by, but never entered. He did tell her he could not afford this place; Whitney, however, laughed lightly and said to not worry, she knew the owner. He learned later that night the owner was her father.

As Michael and Whitney got to know each other that night, he found the attraction meter leaning more and more towards the positive. Whitney was okay. She was bright, intelligent and it appeared she possessed a sense of humor. As their relationship progressed in the future,

Michael realized Whitney was very spoiled; he brushed this to the side since she did grow up with silver spoons as her teething rings. Besides, she was very generous with her money and did not care that Michael came from a middle class family that lived from paycheck to paycheck. The recurring theme was that Whitney had to be in charge. She usually made the decisions and would pout if anyone or anything thwarted them. Her temper would flare hotly and quickly whenever she was crossed. Again, Michael contributed this to her being used to getting her way and pretty much ignored it. He decided he could live with this minor flaw in view of how generous she was financially and how she took the burden of decision making from him. In addition, she acted and spoke as if she adored Michael. His friends teased him and told him he was just her "boy toy", but Michael did not care. While they were drinking beer and teasing him, he was drinking champagne, driving sports cars, sitting in box seats at the ballgames and had an open invitation to the most prestigious clubs and social events in the town. Maybe curly brown haired, tawny colored eyes, petite was a better alternative to tall, slim, blue-eyed blondes.

Due to Whitney's aggressiveness strong willed behavior, the couple had a whirlwind courtship. Before Michael knew what had happened, he was figuratively, Mr. Michael "Springfield" even though they were known as Mr. & Mrs. Michael Smith. Seven months to the day they met, Michael and Whitney were wed. Instinct told Michael this was too soon, but he chalked these thoughts up to male fear of commitment. One fear Michael had not ignored was the fear his father-in-law would want him to join him in the corporate world. Though Michael's job was simple and fairly low in pay, he liked being an in-store plains clothes detective. He felt truly himself in this position and he felt his most self-confident. He was very relieved when neither Mr. Springfield nor Whitney tried to convince him to quit. It was later he learned his store was one of the secret holdings of the Springfield Industries.

As the marriage progressed, Michael saw more and more of Whitney's temper. When she was pregnant with their first child, she was extremely short-tempered and on more than one occasion, had lashed out at Michael physically. She had taken her fists and pummeled him about the chest and head. Michael had been horrified, but had contributed this to hormonal swings. Besides, afterwards he saw some softness in Whitney to which he was not accustomed. She became tearful and blubbered how sorry she was. Michael heard some women became more compliant and some more aggressive so he chalked it up to it being his luck to have a more aggressive pregnant spouse. He figured he could survive this for a few months; anyway, she was not that big physically and her punches did not hurt that badly.

After their son was born, Whitney became less physically violent; her verbal lashings, nevertheless, increased. Michael viewed this as postpartum and spent time protecting the baby from hearing the anger. Within two years, Whitney was pregnant again with their second child. Michael braced himself for nine months of terror and worried how to protect their firstborn. Surprisingly, and much to his relief, Whitney was totally different with this pregnancy. She was cheerful and easygoing. Michael had never seen her this complacent even while they were dating. He fervently wished and prayed this would last. Life was like a "Norman Rockwell" well loved painting. Whitney was the cheerful mommy-to-be and Michael was the breadwinner. They were sharing in the raising of their son and would have family dinners each night. Michael decided the last four years of their marriage had just been an adjustment period, Whitney needed to get all of her abrasive assertiveness out and her first pregnancy had merely been unfortunately, hard.

When Whitney gave birth to their daughter, she had some difficulty and the doctor suggested a tubal ligation. He was not certain if her body would be able to take the strain of carrying and giving birth to another child. Whitney was happy to agree for she did not want more children anyway. Michael was so relieved this pregnancy had been easy, they had their boy and girl and so he too did not argue. He was so happy that they had their All-American family, albeit a little more well off due to her parents.

When Whitney got home with the baby daughter, Michael's son was thrilled. He thought she was a toy and handled her as if she was one of his more precious toys. Michael was happy to think they might not have the horrifying sibling rivalry that frequently occurred in families. Down through the years, he would become more and more grateful for the siblings being close-knit and protective of each other.

As the family settled into being a family, Michael noted signs of Whitney's aggressiveness returning. She would snap at the toddler and pre-schooler for little things—they were giggling too loudly or they stayed in the bathtub too long. When he would address this with her, she would turn on him and tell him she knew what she was doing. She had been raised by a nanny and knew how to raise children. She, in fact, was furious with him for his refusal to let their children be raised by a nanny. Her anger and fury increased almost daily until one day, she slapped Michael again for daring to question her authority with the children. Michael had not been questioning her authority; he was only asking why she seemed so intimidating with them. In addition, he asked in the privacy of their room; not in front of the children. It took all Michael had to not strike back; he, however, was raised to never hit a woman. As previously, Whitney immediately became compliant and apologetic and they began their red rose phase again. This became a cycle.

While David was being judgmental of Michael, he would never know how this seemingly "had it all" guy was being humiliated and physically beaten at home by his wife. As a matter of fact, the general world would never believe it so even if David knew it, his fifteen-year old mind probably could not have comprehended it.

CHAPTER FOURTEEN

David & Daniella: Courtship

By the time David had turned fifteen, he and Daniella had been 'an item' for two years. He could not believe how time passed and neither could she.

The young couple had spent lots of time with their friends, Summer and Nelson. By now, they had added Dawn to their group, too, though she did not come along as often. Dawn was very sweet; she, nevertheless, always seemed reserved and anxious. She spent a lot of time in the bathroom and never wanted anyone to accompany her. David thought this strange because it was his belief system that girls like to go to the bathroom together and gossip. Frankly, Daniella viewed it as Dawn being very private and had no concerns one way or the other. David did not focus on this since it was not really that important to him. He was much more interested in Daniella. He still saw her as the most important and gorgeous person alive.

David and Daniella did spend some time alone, especially now that they were getting older. David finally legally had his driver's permit so he usually did all of the driving, though he still had to drive Daniella's car. This made him feel masculine and in control and it resulted in Daniella feeling taken care of. Since her parents had never spent time taking care of her and showing her affection, she was fully taken with David and the way he 'fussed' over her.

As time passed and hormones fluctuated, David and Daniella inevitably began experimenting more and more in the realms of physical intimacies with each other. This added an entirely different level of emotions to their relationship. Even though they genuinely loved each other as much as they could at their ages, they were not really emotionally capable to handle this type of relationship.

When the relationship blossomed into full intercourse, the couple began fighting. Suddenly, there were trust issues on both sides. Accusations of each other flew and suspicions abounded. Daniella would tearfully accuse David of being more interested in a "prettier" female or one who was his age or one who he did not think he had to steal for to please. David would accuse Daniella of being too provocative around men and that she was flirting with her eyes. He would tell her she thought she could "buy" anyone she wanted. Daniella would accuse David of only being with her because she would sleep with him or she had money.

This really infuriated David for he was such a control freak, he did not even want Daniella to have money. Her reminding him of it would only serve to emasculate him. These infuriating arguments would often lead David to engaging in some unethical activity and cause Daniella to become withdrawn and cold as she perceived her parents to be. Of course, these incidences did not endure for long periods; the problem was they occurred frequently. Both David and Daniella was too young to realize the intensity of their emotions and the adult behavior in which they were engaging were the triggers to these incidents.

In between arguments, David and Daniella were as tight as ever. They continued to spend time alone and with friends. When things were too intense, one or the other would declare they were broken up, but this seldom lasted more than seventy-two hours. Amazingly enough, in that seventy-two hours, one or the other would inevitably go on a date with someone else with the intention being to create jealousy within the other. This did nothing for the trust issues, but they always made up. As would be expected, there were several potential pregnancy scares. By the time Daniella turned eighteen and David turned sixteen, there was a positive pregnancy test.

Daniella had shared with Dawn and Summer her suspicion that she thought she was pregnant. Dawn did her usual and ran to the bathroom. Summer inquired if she was sure and suggested they get home pregnancy tests. They actually purchased four different types. All four said "positive". Summer asked Daniella if they (Daniella & David) did not use birth control and

Daniella assured her they had. Reality hit the teens really hard when they realized it was true: nothing was 100 per cent, except abstinence. Questions swirled in the air: What was Daniella going to do? When would she tell David? In fact, what would she tell David? Daniella knew immediately she would never abort. Placing the baby for adoption was also out of the question because she had always felt abandoned by her parents as she went from one foster home to another and one juvenile detention to another. She was now eighteen and she would be graduating in two months. Daniella was so scared; yet, she felt this might be a way she could finally have the family she wanted. She loved David and no matter how much they fought, she believed David loved her. He had two more years of school, at least she hoped this was all since he often skipped. Daniella had money so she knew she could support the baby. Her parents had provided a college fund for her. She figured she could use this and go to school because she also would have access to the trust fund to which she was entitled at age twenty-one. Daniella began to feel better and was preparing to get up her nerve to approach David.

Daniella called David that night and told him she needed to speak with him. Summer was by her side to give her emotional support. David did not even hesitate to make arrangements to meet her. He had not seen Daniella in about four days and to him that seemed like a lifetime. They arranged to meet up at a local fast food restaurant in an hour or so. He did think it strange that Daniella insisted he not bring Nelson this time. Then being male, he took as a sign she wanted to be with him.

Upon arrival, he saw Daniella sitting dejectedly in their usual booth. When David joined her, he could not determine what the look was on her face. He had never seen this look before and it frightened him. When he inquired what the problem was, she stuttered and suddenly tears gushed from her eyes. All calm, reasonable plans she had made fled from her mind and she blurted "I'm, I'm, I'm Pregnant!" Stating it gave Daniella a sudden feel of calm and confidence until David jumped up and demanded who was the father. Daniella was flabbergasted. What did he mean who was the father? Obviously, it was he. Daniella jumped up from the table without even thinking about her actions and slapped him. David grabbed her wrists and said he had to know; it could not be his because they always used protection.

Interestingly enough, Daniella bad chosen to tell David before telling her parents so as to have their plan ready to present when she told them. She could not believe he was responding this way. she was so furious she could not see straight. Right now, she did not even want David to be the father. Her baby was entitled to a father who was better than this infantile moron. Daniella jumped up from the table, knocking over her chair as she went and drove as fast as she could to Summer's. David stared, still dumbfounded, and finally pulled himself together enough to walk home.

When Daniella arrived at Summer's house, Summer knew immediately that David had not taken it well. This was the reason she attempted to stay away from relationships. It seemed to her, based on her friends, guys always left you high and dry; especially when serious issues as pregnancy arose. Summer had seen friend after friend get pregnant and get dumped. She had sat with many girls in abortion clinics and had watched others lose their adolescence to motherhood. She wanted no part of this and thus, was contented to "just be friends". This explained to a degree, as well, why she was so patient with and receptive to Nelson.

(Summer)

Though Summer had appeared well adjusted, she actually had some subconscious issues going on with her. She did not date not because not only had she not found anyone interesting or trusting enough, but simply because she really did not trust guys at all. Her mother and father had divorced when she was in elementary school and she had loved being with her mom. Her mother did not prevent her from having a relationship with her father, but her father often was "unavailable". In addition, being around her mother and her line of work, Summer had a poor concept of relationships. All of her mother's work revolved around dysfunctional issues. Besides her job, her mom, also, did not date or remarry as her father had done. All of this had begun forming in Summer's subconscious, leading her to believe relationships probably were not the route to go. She, thus, avoided all male interactions that appeared to be of a romantic, commitment issue. She did not have a true role model of how to interact with guys and she did not want pregnancy and heartbreak as so many of friends had. Again and again, she would reflect on her mother's life; she and her mother were close and so for her mother to absolutely stay away from romantic relationships convinced Summer there was something wrong with being involved with males. She had no idea her mom had simply needed to recover from her previous marriage and that she did not want Summer to be introduced to a line of men that were not permanent fixtures in her life. If her mom had known this was the message she was sending to Summer, she would have been more recognizant and responsible in discussing the positive sides of relationships with her. She would not have wanted her daughter to miss out on the joys of teen dating and learning how to have an appropriate, fun loving relationship with the opposite sex.

This, however, is the very thing that formed Summer's attitude about the opposite sex. With the numerous friends with whom she had seen go through bad times and now her best friend, Daniella, Summer was convinced she had made the right decision. Because of this, Summer ended up being well into her twenties before she ever experienced love.

(David)

David was so angry with Daniella for being pregnant. He responded unreasonably as if it was only Daniella's fault. He tried to convince himself it could not be his fault, rationalizing that they always used protection. David, however, was not stupid and he, too, knew no protection was one hundred percent. In his heart of hearts, also knew

Daniella would never cheat on him. Yes, they fought, but he knew she loved him and was the best thing that ever happened to him. She and Nelson were the two people that always showered him with unconditional love and acceptance. In spite of this heart knowledge, David acted on his fear and tried to deny the whole matter. He began seeking the company of others and avoiding Daniella. When Nelson would inquire when they would see Daniella and Summer again, David would gruffly rebuff him and tell him he needed to know girls could not be trusted. Nelson was delayed, but even he knew this did not sound right about Daniella, so he would question and question him repeatedly.

By the time summer rolled around, Daniella was a high school graduate, but she was also three months pregnant. David kept trying to deny it, but he knew the baby was his. Even before he would fully admit it to Daniella, he began seeking work. He was now sixteen and could get legitimate jobs. He knew he needed to work not only for Daniella now, but for the baby, too. Daniella having her own money was still a pride issue for David and he was determined to be "his own man". Without telling her, he acquired a job with a local moving company. He had thought this would be a good stable job, making good money. He could develop his muscular body even more, be outside a lot and meet lots of people. Much to his dismay, he soon learned this was a job that was an "as needed basis". Despite this, he worked fairly steadily and was even able to get the company to let Nelson work some, too.

With his cycle of anger and frustration and then acceptance and resignation, David made some contact with Daniella. He, primarily, however, continued to seek out other girls. He had a hard time admitting to himself it was not the same and he really wanted to be with Daniella.

CHAPTER FIFTEEN

The Self-Mutilator

One day, when in his angry mood, David was doing a moving job where he met Laurie. Laurie's family was moving here from a smaller town, which was only about thirty miles away. It was still considered local, so David was able to work this job. The owner of the moving company did not allow his part time teen employees to do long distance moves.

David met Laurie at the new house. When they arrived at the family's previous home, all, but Mr. Fisher were already at the new home. David, thus, had no idea he would be meeting Laurie. When the moving van pulled up to the obviously middle class home, David felt good about it. He liked seeing some of the fancier homes, but he always left feeling despondent and inferior. This family looked very much as if they would be in the same social circles as his family. David felt at home here and as if he would not be looked down upon. He, rather cockily, began unloading the family's possessions and taking them in when he met her. There standing in the doorway was Laurie. David was immediately drawn to her for she was nothing like Daniella. He needed someone different from Daniella.

Laurie was about 5'5", with a slim build, short, black, wavy hair with black eyes and deep brown skin. When she smiled, he noted she had deep dimples, as well. She was not breathtaking nor curvaceous like Daniella. She appeared rather shy; yet, she did not 'show' any nervousness being in David's presence. David liked this and flirted with her the whole time he was moving the family's possessions. By the end of the move, he had asked her out and she had quietly agreed to going out with him later in the week. They would go to a movie and maybe, out to eat afterwards.

After David left, Laurie felt breathless that this good-looking guy would notice her. She had made a conscious effort to appear nonchalant and unaffected by his presence, but inside she was a quivering bowl of jelly. She made plans as to what to wear for their date and was really looking forward to it. As the night of the date drew near, however, Laurie's anxiety skyrocketed. This was not first date jitters, Laurie was almost paralyzed with anxiety. To calm herself, Laurie engaged in her secret way of handling things. She was hoping if David and she hit it off, she either stop this or he would never find out.

Laurie was the third of four children. She had two older sisters and one younger brother. Her eldest sister was gorgeous, a total knockout. She, in fact was enrolled in a modeling school when she was sixteen and now that she was twenty, had landed a few minor modeling jobs at nearby department stores. Her second oldest sister was the brain of the family. She had made straight A's in school, while barely cracking a book. In fact, this past May when she graduated from school, she was the valedictorian of her class. As for her brother, well, just being the only boy and the youngest made him special. At age thirteen, he was already getting attention from girls and he played on the school's basketball team. Laurie felt she had no special characteristics. She was average looking, an average student and not a boy. She often felt lost in the shuffle of this family. She had found her special coping activity was the only thing that gave her both a sense of control and released the pent-up anxiety. Laurie took a deep breath and tried to talk herself down, but it did not work. She had to release the pain in order to keep her date with David.

When David arrived the night of the date, no one would have ever known the stress Laurie had been under. She had on blue jeans, a bright yellow pullover shirt with blue jean covered, high-heeled sandals. Even with her three-inch heels and five foot five height, David still towered over her. By now, he was over six feet tall. Laurie was bowled over by him and could not believe he had asked her out. Mentally, she repeated her mantra to herself to be calm and just enjoy the evening.

When she arrived back home after the hilarious movie and nice meal after the movie, she was tickled she had made it through the evening. Though he had not acted overly excited, David did seem to like her and he had asked her out again. She had heard rumors from her new neighbors that David was involved with a gorgeous girl and she was pregnant. David, however, had not mentioned this and she did not want to rock the boat by inquiring. She decided to let sleeping dogs lie.

The next morning, Laurie was still excited from the previous night. For the first time in several months, she felt no desire to engage in her secret coping behavior because her emotions were no longer numb; she felt alive, very alive. She actually sang as she showered and initiated casual conversation with her family members. They were all surprised, but were so relieved to see Laurie seemingly to feel confident and to be behaving in a more outgoing manner than they had ever seen Mrs. Fisher decided it was the move here, but Mr. Fisher felt a gnawing anxiety in his stomach, which told him that it was "the boy" causing her to act this way. This resulted in myriad thoughts: he was glad someone brought that girl out of her dark cloud, but he was a dad so he also felt panic about his daughter's reaction to a boy. No matter how many daughters he raised, it always stressed him when their interest in the opposite sex was peaked. Laurie's sisters teased her about her big grin and poked at her, as sisters will do. Her brother was oblivious to her.

Laurie waited for the phone to ring all day, but David never called. This put somewhat of a damper on her mood, but it did not obliterate her current sunny disposition. She read 'Teen' and 'Young Miss' so she knew guys often waited to call so they would not look desperate. She rode high on her memories of the night before, all day. As he drifted off to sleep that night, she had a smitten grin all over her face and she, of course, dreamt of David.

The next morning, Laurie again had buoyancy in her steps and a fluttering in her heart. She was sure David would call today. She wondered if she could convince her parents to let her stay home from church in case he called. Laurie felt so good, however, she could not fake illness and she knew nothing short of "near death" would her parents allow her to miss church. She, thus, got dressed for church and sat through the whole service, praying David would not call until she got home.

By ten that night, David had not called. The old desire to use her secret coping method began creeping in Laurie's mind and heart. Her family noticed the familiar depressed look and began worrying. They did not know what was going on with Laurie, but knew she was not happy. Her sisters assumed it was David and tried to encourage her by telling her this was typical guy behavior and had nothing to do with her. Her mom resorted to talking with her dad and allowing him to convince her Laurie was being a typical teen. Her mom really felt it was different, but wanted so very much to believe her husband was right, she let it go. The whole family would have been very distressed had they known how deep this "perceived rejection" was to the sensitive young lady. Around midnight, when all was quiet in the Fisher home, Laurie tiptoed lightly to the bathroom, pulled out her secret weapon—her razor—and repeatedly dragged it across her inner thigh until she drew blood, felt the excruciating pain and then the surge of power, as she knew she could determine how long she felt this pain. After the initial rush and relief, Laurie was able to bandage the thigh, tiptoe back to bed and sleep fairly soundly for the rest of the night.

While Laurie was torturing herself physically and emotionally, David was actually thinking about her. He had decided since he had no moving jobs the next day, he would call her and see if she wanted to "do something". He wasn't sure what since he was still trying to avoid running into Daniella. This placed limits where the couple could spend time. As David thought about this, his thoughts turned to Daniella. He had caught glimpses of her over the weekend. In fact, he and Nelson had been 'hanging out', and he had been thinking of calling Laurie when he saw her. This was actually why he did not call her the day after their date. He had been so amazed at Daniella's swollen stomach; yet she still looked so gorgeous. He knew within his heart of hearts this baby was his and he knew he had to confront reality eventually. For now, though, he was going to try to avoid reality as long as possible. He decided the best way to do this was to work, save money, spend time with Nelson and focus his attention on Laurie.

Laurie awakened with a heavy heart the next morning. David, on the other hand, awakened with plans to call Laurie. Before he could call her, the phone rang and he was being called into work for a few hours. There was a last minute, local moving job arranged and David's boss said he would like for David and Nelson to work it. David, momentarily, thought he would call Laurie anyway and see if she was available that evening.

At the last moment though, he decided to just wait; instead, he called Nelson and arranged to pick him up in the next hour. While this was occurring, Laurie was sinking further and further beneath her covers.

Around 11:00 a.m., as David and Nelson were completing the morning move, Laurie's eldest sister was attempting to coax her out of bed. She offered to take her shopping, do a makeover on her and then maybe go to the movies. Laurie was being resistant to all suggestions. Becoming frustrated and flustered with Laurie's stubbornness, her sister threw her hands up in the air and said "forget it; act stupid if you want over some silly boy you just met". Laurie was feeling badly enough about herself, so decided to at least, go shopping and do the makeover.

While she was taking a shower and letting her tears mingle with the water, Laurie would have felt more buoyant had she known David was dialing her number right then. As she exited the shower, she was feeling a little better when she heard her sister yelling her name. Laurie ignored her, but when she continued to call her, out of exasperation Laurie finally yelled "What?" Laurie moved from despondency to anticipation at the speed of lightening when the response was "David's on the phone for you". Standing dripping wet with a towel barely covering her, Laurie took a deep breath and then answered the phone in a careless tone, "Hello". when she heard David's deep baritone voice, she thought she would actually melt into nothingness. He was asking her if she would be interested in hanging out later. He suggested going to the local skating rink and if she liked, pick up some Chinese food. Laurie quietly agreed outwardly; inwardly, she was screaming and jumping up and down. Hanging up, she told her sister she definitely needed to shop and have her makeover now. Her sister, feeling somewhat angry at this complete change of attitude over a boy, yet relieved that Laurie was showing life, agreed to help her for her date that night.

For Laurie, the date was a fairy tale. She again felt no need to cut herself that night—just hug herself tightly. She and David already had plans for later that week. Laurie rode high through the week until their next date and did not cut herself one time. She began to think she was someone special after all and her emotions were very much active and not numb.

For the next month and a half, David and Laurie spent more and more time together. Laurie only cut herself two or three times the whole time. She appeared more confident, but what she was actually doing, was becoming dependent on David instead of on the cutting. She began calling him a lot and insisting on knowing where he was all the time. She would call Nelson and ask him where David was. Nelson would answer when he knew because he sort of liked Laurie. Nelson did not understand why she sounded so scared when she would call him though. He had never been around girls who acted like this. Neither Summer nor Daniella had ever done anything like this. Nelson, nevertheless, just went along with the program.

David became somewhat irritated with Laurie for always calling him and for her calling Nelson about him. The final straw for him, however, was when she asked him to wear a pager so she could always find him. When he indicated they were not married and this was stupid, Laurie fell apart before his very eyes. She began howling like a coyote and before David knew what was happening, she had whipped out a razor and was slicing her thighs and arms. David went ballistic. He had never seen anything so bizarre in his life. He wanted to grab the razor, but did not know how without getting cut himself. He finally settled on just grabbing her arm and screaming at her. By then her leg and arm were covered in blood. David knew enough to take her to the emergency room and to call her parents.

Guilt, fear, and confusion plagued David thereafter about Laurie. He wondered if this was all due to his not being with her twenty-four seven. This, however, did not make any sense. When her parents arrived at the hospital and seemed to be just as flabbergasted, David did not feel so dumb. He did know this was a problem that he could not and did not want to deal with, not with anyone. Her parents were devastated as they talked with the E.R. doctor and then were referred to a psychiatrist. They assured David, however, that they knew it had nothing to do with him and were very grateful to him for taking Laurie to the hospital and calling them. They kept telling him how responsible he was. This fed into David's ego and his need to be "somebody", but not to the degree that he wanted to remain involved with Laurie.

David called the Fishers the next day to check on Laurie and learned she was going to be inpatient at a mental health center for adolescents for a while. David still felt slightly responsible; he, however, knew this was the last of his friendship with Laurie. As he reflected on it, he knew she probably felt they were "an item" as he and Daniella had been, and that is why she called so often. He, however, considered her a good female friend to spend time with and to help him forget Daniella. He believed, initially, that the former was accomplishment. He had to admit though, if only to himself, that the latter had not been accomplished in the least. Daniella was like a permanent memory burned in his heart, mind and soul. David did learn a lesson from this; he knew he needed to be more careful with the next female he met. He, also, wanted to ensure he did not become the slightest bit involved with someone as needy as Laurie.

CHAPTER SIXTEEN

The Manipulator

As Danielle's pregnancy progressed, she began experiencing a mixture of emotions. She was hurt by David's response and thus, she and he had very little contact. She had seen him around the town, but she always tried to avoid him. Daniella had heard about his dating other girls and this hurt her almost as much as his denial of fathering her baby. The baby was becoming more and more real to her. She had survived the nauseating first trimester and now she was experiencing the wonder of a growing baby. When she had her first ultrasound, she wanted so badly to call David and share with him, but her pride would not allow her to do this. Maternal instincts, as well as nevertheless, were kicking into high gear. Daniella was afraid to have and raise this baby alone and she wanted her baby to have the knowledge and love of his dad. As anger at David dissipated, her emotional pain expanded: she now felt pain for herself and for the baby. Deep within her heart, she believed David really did love her and was simply being a childish male. She fervently prayed he would overcome his fear and come back to her and the baby. Even though she desperately wanted David back in her life, she was more concerned that he be in the life of the baby, especially since she now knew she was having a boy.

Daniella often talked to Summer and Summer's mom about her predicament. They were both being supportive of her; in fact, Summer's mom is the one who took her to her first obstetric appointment. Her own mom was still too busy running around, being Mrs. Popularity. She expressed distaste about Daniella being pregnant and was really irritated that it was by a male "not of their status". Daniella, thus, had written mom out of the picture and was replacing her with Summer's mom. This still did not fill the void left by David. Daniella was attempting to make tentative plans on how to have David in the baby's life without getting her hopes up that he would be in her life, too. Summer was encouraging her to not focus on David being with her, but to make him accountable as a father. Daniella's emotional pain had not yet allowed her to rid herself of all lingering hope they could be a family, but she was consistent in her decision to ensure the baby did not suffer from lack of a father no matter what did or did not happen with her and David.

As Daniella tried to cope with her pregnancy and emotional pain by leaning on her friend and her friend's mom for support, David tried to deal with his guilt and fear by dating as many other people as he could. What he continued to discover, though, was he was comparing them to Daniella and they always came out on the short end of the stick. He had taken several different girls to the movies and/or to eat out, but it was usually a one time situation. He did not make any efforts to introduce any of them to his family, though he did talk of two of them with his dad. When he finally discussed Daniella with his dad, he did so to inquire why he could not be contented with other girls, specifically—Laurie and a girl named Brooklyn.

Laurie had really scared him and confused him when he learned of Laurie's intense neediness and of her self-mutilating behaviors. He was way too young to understand and handle this. He wanted a girl to look up to and need him, but not stifle him.

When David had survived that brutalizing break up with Laurie, he had immediately sought out someone totally different. That is when he met Brooklyn.

Brooklyn was a cutie pie. She was only five feet tall and was definitely weight/height proportionate. She was a fiery ball of independence and seemed to be a match for David. She did not seem intimidated by him, awed by him or too needy of him. She seemed to be his equal and much to his surprise, he sort of liked this. Brooklyn was a challenge.

David had met Brooklyn while standing in line at the movies. She was dressed outrageously in a flimsy bright red skirt, oversized, almost sheer, off the shoulder, purple, cropped top and three inch heels. Of course, Brooklyn could afford to wear very high heels and still be shorter than David. He was amused at her large hoop earrings dangling down from under her golden brown, long pageboy hairstyle. Brooklyn wore more make-up than most of the girls David knew, but it looked good on her. She was very aggressive with him and in fact, she approached him at the movies. When she found out which movie he and Nelson were going to see, she exchanged her movie ticket so she could be with them. Brooklyn was not as gorgeous as Daniella and she was not as timid as Laurie. David thought maybe this was the girl, however, that could get his mind off of his messy situation with Daniella. It did concern him that Nelson did not seem to care for Brooklyn. Nelson seemed to have an uncanny ability to read people and he would often tell David he did not like him hanging out with Brooklyn. David, nevertheless, had brushed this to the side, assuming Nelson just missed hanging out with Daniella and Summer.

There were many red flags popping up about Brooklyn. On their first date, the one she initiated, Brooklyn insisted they meet at a local pizza joint. She had told David she lived in a really ritzy neighborhood, but that her parents would embarrass her if David picked her up so would not tell him exactly where she lived. She said she had a sports car and could meet him at the restaurant. David had bought a jeep with some of his summer job money so he agreed to meet her. When he arrived, he saw no sports car parked there, so was surprised when Brooklyn was already there. When he inquired about the whereabouts of her car, she said she had to put it in the shop that morning. David asked why she had not called and had him pick her up. She reminded him her parents were just "too embarrassing" and said her friend dropped her off. Since Brooklyn was sixteen, this sounded feasible to David and he shrugged off the nagging thought that her explanation did not really fly.

Brooklyn did not hesitate to tell David what she wanted to eat and actually forced him to dance with her at the pizza joint. She was flirtatious with everyone; yet, it did not seem to bother David. It, instead, attracted and challenged him. Brooklyn had told David she would pay half of the bill, but when time came to pay, she hysterically said she could not find her wallet, let her lower lip quiver while seemingly allowing tears to flow from her eyes and over her cheeks. David assured her this was fine and within a few seconds, Brooklyn was dry-eyed, smiling and suggesting they go to the mall. By the time they left the mall, David realized he had purchased her a whole outfit and did not know how this happened. Brooklyn wanted to then try to sneak into a club with fake I.D.'s, which she produced from the "lost wallet". David told her he did not have any more money to spend so she said she guessed they should call it a night. David assumed he would take her home, but she insisted she was spending the night with a friend and had David drop her off at an unknown house. The friend did not come out when they arrived; Brooklyn jumped out of the jeep, kissed David fully on the lips and then stood on the sidewalk and waved goodbye to him. It was only later that David realized he never saw her walk up to or go into a house. Driving home, David also realized he did not even have her phone number. Brooklyn did the entire calling, all of the initiating and made all of the plans. It, also, struck him then that she had weaseled his phone number from him when they first met, but had never offered her own.

Upon arriving home, David had thoughts of calling Daniella. The date with Brooklyn had only served to make him think of Daniella even more, instead of forgetting her. He, however, was mentally and emotionally exhausted and decided to just go to bed. Falling promptly asleep, he slept well, but when awakening the next morning, reviewed the night previously. It was then he realized how Brooklyn was really taking over and he felt manipulated. He thought to himself that Brooklyn was a total trip and one he decided he did not want to take. At that very moment, the phone rang. Briefly, his fluttered thinking was it might be Daniella. When he answered though, it was Brooklyn. She insisted on going out that day and before he knew it, he had agreed to another date with her. His resolve only minutes earlier to not see her again, flew out the window.

As before, Brooklyn insisted he not pick her up, she would meet him. She wanted to meet at The Gap and David agreed. He intended to ask her for her phone number and to tell her to bring her friend so he could bring Nelson. As usual, Brooklyn was so intense; he forgot to ask.

David actually enjoyed this outing with Brooklyn, but could not shake the unidentifiable nagging beneath the surface he had about her. He could not put his finger on it, but he knew something was awry about both Brooklyn and his quickly growing relationship with her. He mentally shook his head to rid himself of these thoughts, reminding himself how cute and fun she was and how nothing out of the ordinary had occurred on this date.

For the next several days, David neither heard from Brooklyn nor, he realized, had he even thought of trying to contact her; not that he could, since he had no address or phone number. David had been spending most of his time, brooding over Daniella whenever he was not with Nelson or at work.

As he was doing his usual brooding, David almost determined to call Daniella. Instead, he picked up the phone and called Nelson. Much to his dismay, Nelson's grandmother said Nelson was not feeling well and could not come to the phone. David sat down, rather despondently and was again contemplating calling Daniella. Just as he began dialing, he heard someone blowing a car horn. He looked out the window and saw this sleek, black, customized Camaro, parked in front of his house. When he went to the door, Brooklyn bounced out and waved at him. "Come on, let's go". "Go where?", David inquired. "To the mall or something", Brooklyn responded. David was very curious about the car, so he thought "why not?" At least, it would prevent him from making the mistake of giving in and calling Daniella. It also prevented him from wondering how she knew where he lived.

As he was leaving out, he hollered to his mom he was going to the Mall. Mrs. O'Brien stopped him and reminded him she was not the household pet; he was to come to her and speak—not holler at her. With head bowed, feet shuffling, David mumbled an apology. He quickly kissed her on the cheek and told her he was meeting someone at the Mall. Rebecca grabbed his arm and asked if that someone happened to be Daniella. David blushed and said no. she then asked him what did he think he was doing. She knew Daniella was pregnant and she had tried to give David space, but it was time to talk. Irritated and guilty, David asked couldn't it wait, but she said no.

David told his mom he knew Daniella was pregnant, but he was not sure it was his. Mrs. O'Brien could not believe a son of hers would actually behave this way. She told David she knew he did not really believe this and for the first time, David cried. He told his mom he was sorry and just didn't know what to do. His mom hugged him to her bosom and began comforting him. As David was beginning to open up, Brooklyn blew the horn again. David tensed up and the moment was broken. Being a mom, Rebecca sensed David was worried about something. She told him if this was something he really did not want to do, he did not have to do it. The curiosity about the Camaro was tugging at his adolescent male mind, while the desire to talk with his mom was tugging at his emotional state… David was so relieved at mom's help, he decided to briefly tell her about his fears about Daniella, etc… He asked mom if they could talk later and she assured him they could. He had known that at that very moment, Brooklyn was having a mental, hysterical tantrum, he would not have felt so comforted; he would have felt frightened for at that moment, Brooklyn was becoming enraged at David not immediately responding to her horn blowing.

When David finally got in the car, Brooklyn was fuming. She snapped at him with "sit down, shut up and put on your seatbelt". David, taken off guard, was obeying orders, but asked "What is your problem?" Brooklyn simply rolled her eyes at him, caused the tires to squeal as she pulled away from the curb and began mumbling under her breath.

Mrs. O'Brien slowly shook her head and muttered to herself, "this girl is going to be trouble" as she stood in the doorway, witnessing the departure. She had heard David talk about a "Brooklyn" on the phone to Nelson. She had also answered the phone a few times when Brooklyn called, but had never met her. The maternal instinct and the wisdom of age, nevertheless, let her know this girl was "pure Trouble".

Finally, as the couple entered the interstate, Brooklyn was ready to talk. What stirred the red flags for David, however, was she began talking sweetly and cheerfully to him, as if the muttering, ordering and squealing had never occurred. He soon found out why; she said she needed to pay her pager bill, but realized she had not brought enough money. Batting her eyes at him, she softly asked "David, can you help me out? I need to pay my pager bill at the mall and don't have enough money". David stared at her, dumbfounded. This girl's moods were too swift for him to handle and she always managed to con him into spending money on her. He remembered concurrently, it was usually when she had convinced him to go out, too; it was never his asking her out. As he mulled this over, Brooklyn's "jekyll and hyde" personality switched again into high gear. Snapping at him, the question again arose "Can you help me out or not???" Before David could respond, a poor guy had the misfortune of making the mistake of pulling out from an exit onto the interstate in front of Brooklyn. She slammed her brakes, then sped up, spewing choice phrases about how ugly cars should not be allowed on the road. She felt like she should just slam into his rear end and teach him a lesson. She yelled at David, "What idiot would drive a puke green Yugo? They should not be allowed on the road. It would serve him right and do him a favor if she just totaled the piece of junk for him." David felt fear rise from his dropped heart into his throat. This girl was nuts!! Her ranting and raging about the car did remind him why he had agreed to come with her—he wanted to know about the dream machine she was driving. David tried to calm her by telling her he was glad to be with her, would help her pay her pager bill and for her to not let some unknown guy ruin their day. Brooklyn slowed down, grinned at him and blew him a kiss. "You are so right! You and I have better things to do", she suggested in a husky voice.

As they pulled off the exit to the mall, David inquired "how do you adjust the bass on this CD player?" Brooklyn shrugged, "how would I know? The manual is in the arm rest". David briefly wondered why she would not know this about her own car, but decided it was a 'girl thing'. As be rummaged through the armrest, he noticed the registration. It had a male name listed. David asked "who is Jerome?" "Why?", Brooklyn growled. "I thought this was the sports car you had told me about when we first met, but the registration is in a guy's name". David then burst out in a sweat and asked "Is this car stolen?" He had been in enough trouble without adding this to his list of violations. Brooklyn threw back her head, swinging her curls and almost guffawed, "Please!" Without giving any further explanation, she said "give me the money so I can pay my bill and I'll be right back". David handed her the money, but was fuming while she was inside. He even had the thought of driving off and leaving her. She had left the keys in the car. Reality, however, set in and he remembered he did not even know whose car this was. Anyway, by this time, Brooklyn was bouncing back to the car; jumped in, pulled his face to hers and kissed him fully on the lips. "You are sooo sweet. Now my bill is paid, you can page me anytime, anywhere for any reason".

David, baffled by these swift and frequent changes, looked at her and then calmly asked, "Brooklyn, who is Jerome and if this is his car, where is he?" "He's nobody now", she said. "What do you mean, he is nobody now?" Brooklyn let her convenient tears flow, while her lips quivered and spoke very quietly and shyly, "I did not know how to tell you. I was hoping I would never have to tell you. Jerome is my boyfriend". "WHAT?" David countered. He broke out in a sweat and began nervously looking around as if the guy was near and witnessing this. Brooklyn noticing the reaction, switched to caregiver, stating, "it's okay, baby; he's in jail". David countered again with "WHAT?" "J-A-I-L, David! The S.O.B. hit me and I had him arrested, okay? He'll be gone for awhile so don't worry about it". David, totally, stunned, stared at Brooklyn and said "he hit you?" David had done a lot of things in his short life, but he would never consider laying his hand on a female in anger. This angered her and she asked if he wanted to see the bruises and scars that would never leave as she began tugging at her blouse. David shook his head "no" and said he was sorry he asked. Brooklyn laid her head on David's shoulder and cried like a baby. She kept saying "I'm sorry". David said "there is never an excuse for a man to hit a woman and you have no need to apologize". David did not realize how Brooklyn had totally redirected his attention and not only were they not going to the mall as the original plan was, she was asking if they could just go home because she was so upset by the memories.

When arriving home, David felt such pity and sorrow for this unknown factor of this 'helpless' creature, he hugged and kissed her bye. He never saw the gleam in her eye or the gloating on her face as she pulled away. If he had known the real stories of both their trip today and the boyfriend, he would have been full of rage. Initially, David felt sorry for Brooklyn and had forgotten her wild mood swings. When he recalled the afternoon later, however, and realized not only had she not answered any questions, he remembered she said she had a boyfriend—one in jail, nonetheless. In addition, he suddenly he realized that he had gone from "helping her pay her pager bill" to paying the whole bill AND they had done nothing else. She had "used" him to the fullest. David thought to himself, "it is time to leave her alone".

(Brooklyn)

Brooklyn had arrived earlier that day in the car deliberately. She knew David was a sucker for sports cars. She knew this would make him go riding with her. Her only plan had been for him to pay her pager bill. She had not intended to share any information about the car, but she had slipped by him look for that stupid manual. This, in itself, would have disturbed David. After all, part of David's delinquent behavior had occurred due to his need to not be controlled.

David never learned—and Brooklyn was planning to ensure he never would—the truth about her boyfriend. The reason she never let David take her home was because she did not live with "wealthy parents", as she told David; she lived with her boyfriend. Brooklyn had actually grown up in foster care until she turned sixteen. That was when she met and moved in with the suave Jerome. Her parents were never there for her. She did not know her father and her mother was constantly bringing in one man after another. When the men were around, her mother would insist she call them "uncle" or "daddy". They would give her what she wanted so she would leave them alone with her mother. Later, as she got older, the men would leer and grope at her. Her mother, when not with men, would simply drink and drink and drink. She would not get Brooklyn ready for school, buy groceries or do anything a responsible parent should. A concerned teacher, when she was about twelve, noticed her disheveled appearance, her always sleeping in class and never having her work completed. This is what got her in and out of foster care. The last foster home had not been too bad. It had taught her how to dress to attract guys and get what she wanted. What it did not teach her, Jerome did.

Having seen how her mom was around men and how she ignored Brooklyn when there was a man in her life, Brooklyn had decided then and there, no man would run over her. At this point, she had not even seen her mom in several years. She assumed she was either with some man or falling down drunk somewhere. She might even be dead, but Brooklyn told herself she did not care one way or the other.

When Brooklyn met Jerome, she had been flattered by his attention. He taught her how to dress, took her out and told her she was beautiful. When she began developing feelings, it scared her, so she decided to take control of him. Jerome was elder by four years, actually worked and seemed to genuinely care for her. Brooklyn, though did not know how to handle caring feelings and she, thus, tested him constantly. She deliberately started fights, would call him names, and often left claw marks down his face and back and arms where she had attacked him. She told David she had scars and had been relieved when he did not demand to see them. She had not figured out how she would have handled that since she had no marks anywhere on her body.

Jerome was in jail, but it was a false arrest. As usual, Brooklyn had been accusing him of cheating, of not caring about her and had gone into one of her rages. When Jerome tried to protect himself from her, he had put his hands out in front of him and when she pummeled into them, she fell back and hit the floor. She then called the police and told them Jerome had attacked and pushed her. When the police questioned if they had been arguing, Jerome, flabbergasted at this turn of events, admitted they had. When he tried to explain what happened, Brooklyn had turned on the whimpering, helpless act and the police arrested Jerome for domestic violence. Actually, Brooklyn felt really bad about this after it happened, but did not know how to correct it. She genuinely cared for Jerome, but did not know how to handle this this foreign feeling of love nor how to deal with the consequences of her impulsive behaviors. After all, she was just a teenager. All of this had actually occurred a couple of days before she met David. In order to not deal with it, she had latched onto David when she met him to help her not think about Jerome.

After deciding to leave Brooklyn alone David was dismayed to find over the next several days, there were numerous calls from Brooklyn. Since he was working that week, he managed to avoid her. He did become concern when notes of love and begging, appeared on his car windshield. Not only did this indicate that he was being watched, but he became aware Brooklyn had to be furious and in a rage when he began having unexplainable flat tires, as well as scratch marks on the doors of his jeep. David thought about his original instinct that Brooklyn might be dangerous as well as the fact that Nelson really disliked her. He did not know how to prove it was her doing these things, though. Not for the first time, he wondered what he had gotten himself into with her. David knew he had to confront Brooklyn and talk about this. He realized again, nevertheless, that he had no idea how to reach her—he still did not have an address or phone number for her or even her pager number though paid the bill. He suddenly remembered their first date and the house where he dropped her—he would go there.

David found his way back to Brooklyn's "phantom friend's" house. He had never met "this friend", but decided to take his chances. He went up to the door where he thought she probably went. Was he ever surprised when a white haired lady answered the door. He asked for Brooklyn; this lady said there was no Brooklyn there—just her and her husband. She said her children were all grown and none of them were named Brooklyn. David apologized to the lady and left.

Not knowing what else to do, David decided he should ride around the neighborhood in hopes of spotting Brooklyn. He did not see her after about forty-five minutes and decided to go home. Much to his surprise, when he arrived home, Brooklyn was sitting on his porch. David felt both relief and fear at the sight of her.

Making an effort to appear unflustered and nonchalant, David swaggered up his front door and casually said "hey". His heart was beating overtime and his palms were sweaty for he knew though he appeared calm, he was scared. He had only been on a real date with Brooklyn a couple of times, but her constant calling and showing up in unexpected places caused him to feel as if he knew her much better. Brooklyn stared wide-eyed at David and demanded to know where he had been. Before he even realized what was happening, David found himself trying to account for why he had not been calling. Suddenly, reality hit him and he told Brooklyn they were "just friends". He reminded her they were not a "couple". David told Brooklyn he knew she was sabotaging his possessions and the ceaseless calling had to stop. Brooklyn switched tactics; she then glanced at David from underneath half closed lids, with her long lashes spreading out like a feathery duster on her face. She allowed her lips to quiver and forced a tear from one eye. Brooklyn told David she was so sorry; it was just she liked him so much and she just wanted to spend time with him. Brooklyn slowly sat down on the porch, put her head in her hands and her shoulders shook as she appeared to be sobbing.

David tried to remain hard, but softened and sat next to her. He put his arms around her, laid his chin on her head and told her it would be all right. He told her they could be friends if she would let him call her sometimes and give him some space. Amazingly enough, Brooklyn looked up completely dry eyes, a dazzling smile eagerly agreed. Immediately after agreeing she asked David if they could go out that night. David stared at her in disbelief. He could not believe only moments ago she was acting distraught, then agreeable and then doing exactly what he had asked her not to do. He felt like a fly in a spider web. Not knowing what to do, he agreed to a movie that night.

After the movie, David again realized he did enjoy Brooklyn's company, but he also was beginning to mature; he, thus, was having some confusion with which to deal. He knew he did not want to be in a relationship with Brooklyn. He knew no matter how many one time dates, how much bravado he showed and how much he avoided, at the tender age of sixteen, he knew he loved Daniella AND he was going to be a father. This was more than the average adult male could handle and as teen, it was even more distressing.

CHAPTER SEVENTEEN

David—Growing Up

Later that evening, David had been zoned out in front of the television when his father came home. His father had been on the road for several days and was exhausted. When Mr. O'Brien, however, saw the dejection his son seemed to be feeling, he put that exhaustion aside and went to speak with him. David looked up with sad eyes, mumbled hello and went back to staring blankly at the television. Mr. O'Brien went to his wife, greeted her and then asked what was up with David. She shared briefly about their conversation. Mr. O'Brien returned to David.

When John walked back into the living room and David still did not look up, he talked in front of the television screen, turned it off and softly called to David, "son, you looking kind of down. Anything you want to talk about?" David said "naw, dad", but John would not give up. He inserted a video game onto the set and he and his son began to play. As John intended, during the game, David began to talk.

David reminded John of when he had asked him earlier about why he could not be contented with other girls. John talked to David about the fact that you cannot always choose with whom you fall in love. He told David that though he felt David was too young for love, maybe David really needed to examine what he really felt for everyone involved. He did admonish David that no matter what, he had the responsibility of being a father. He told him it was time to face that reality and assured him he and mom would both be there to help David and Daniella. He reminded him this would be their grandbaby and they would do all they could. David needed to remember, however, he was the dad and this was his responsibility.

David stopped playing the game, looked up with understanding clarity as he suddenly experienced an epiphany. David knew that though he was very young according to the world's standards, he was old enough to know what he felt. He loved Daniella, he was in love with her and furthermore, he liked her. He enjoyed the dependence from Laurie for a short time; he enjoyed the flamboyance of Brooklyn for a night out and he enjoyed having friends to go to the movies, ballgames, mall, to eat, etc… It, however, was Daniella that he wanted to talk to; share good and bad times with and just sit around sometimes doing nothing. No matter how many other girls he hung out with, kissed, hugged and flirted with, no one could compare to both the excitement and comfort he felt in Daniella's presence. Moreover, as scary as it was and as much as he had run from it, Daniella was having his baby. This baby was a part of her and him. He did not know how to handle it and he did not really want to handle it, but he knew he did not want anyone else with Daniella. For the second time that day, and much to the humiliating relief of the teen, tears flowed down his cheeks. His father again offered assurance and reassurance. David gave his dad rough and awkward hug and said he thought it was time to try to make up with Daniella. Mr. O'Brien was totally relieved. He was sorry David had such heavy responsibilities at such a tender age, but he liked Daniella. If this had to happen, he was glad it was with a girl he believed David really loved and one that he and Mrs. O'Brien liked as well. As David left the room, John O'Brien sat down with a sigh and thought about the fact that he was going to be a "grandfather". He then uttered up a silent prayer that Daniella would forgive David and that the young people would be able to work this out.

(David & Daniella)

After talking with his dad and accepting some of his emotional distress and reality, David was completely worn out. He stretched out in bed, making plans to contact Daniella the next morning. He knew he would have to somehow stop Brooklyn from bugging him, but overall, he felt such peace-for the first time in months. David had always been raised to pray, so he offered up his own prayers that God would be with him, help him to talk to Daniella and help him to be a good daddy, whatever that meant. He then slept soundly throughout the night.

The next morning, David awakened with a start. He felt slightly disoriented and experienced anxiety and anticipation simultaneously. Looking around and familiarizing himself anew with his room, her tried to remember what had happened the previous night. That was when he had his moment of clarity and recalled his conversations with mom, dad and Brooklyn. He had determined he would be calling Daniella today. This decision was what was evoking these mixed emotions.

David reached for the phone and then decided he would shower and brush his teeth first. This would serve as a two-fold purpose. If Daniella was receptive to his coming over, he would already be ready and it would give him time to calm himself. While showering and dressing, David hummed to himself and rehearsed in his mind what to say. Finally, with no more distractions, David again reached for the phone but his hand remained in a paralyzed position. He was scared. He reminded himself this was just Daniella. He attempted to assuage his guilt by telling himself that Daniella was just as responsible for her pregnancy as he was. He denied his cowardly behavior and justified it by thinking she could have called him; maybe, she was guilty because maybe she really thought the baby was not his. David physically shook his head to rid himself of these negative thoughts. He shook his hand up and down to ensure they were not really in a state of paralysis—just fear.

Shifting his thoughts, shaking himself loose and mentally rehearsing again what to say, he dialed her number before he froze again. After no answer on the third ring. David felt sweat pouring down his freshly showered armpits and face. He had decided he could not go through with it, when he heard that familiar sweet, heartrending, never forgotten voice of his love. It was as if it was the first time he had called her and heard her. His voice caught in his throat and he could not even force out a response. After Daniella had said "hello", about three times, and was obviously about to hang up, David squeaked out a "hey". It was now Daniella's turn to freeze up and become silent. The silence lasted so long, both began to fear the other had disconnected. Then, at the exact same moment in time, both whispered respectively, "Daniella?" "David?" Of course, they both went silent again; then Daniella dropped her pride and with tearfulness, said "oh, David". For the third time in two days, David felt tears rush down his face as he told Daniella, "I am so sorry for the way I have acted. I love you! I want to make up for being so dumb. Can I please see you?" Daniella sent up a silent prayer of thanks and told him to come on over.

Daniella fussed over what to wear. She was so big with pregnancy; yet she was still concerned what David would think. She called Summer who told her she hoped all went well, but cautioned her to be careful. They then talked about what Daniella should wear. Daniella finally settled on a baby doll looking maternity tops and shorts. Despite the fully rounded belly, she still looked good. Though David loved her in red, his favorite color was green, so she had chosen a green and red checked top with the green shorts. She put on flat red sandals to cope with her often, swelling feet. She did not know for sure if she was flushed from pregnancy, heat or excitement. Regardless, she thought it best to keep the cooling, baby powder near while she sat under the air conditioner. She then pulled her dark hair, which had grown even longer during pregnancy into a high ponytail, tied with a green bow. Despite the tight ponytail, her hair still swung low down her back. She then waited what felt like hours to her, but was actually only thirty minutes, for David to arrive.

David had told his parents where he was going; had called Nelson and told him he would see him later. Nelson was so excited to learn he was going to see Daniella. He kept saying, "Nelson love David and Daniella. Nelson gonna be an uncle". After the approval of both his parents and Nelson, David felt like this was old times and things would be okay.

Arriving at Daniella's, David lost the familiar comfort and felt his heart beating so rapidly and loudly, he was afraid the neighbors would hear. He took deep breaths, mentally and physically shook himself and ran up the steps to Daniella's. He, briefly, worried her parents would answer. Since he did not know their response, he wondered if they would curse him, slam the door in his face or threaten him in some way. This was a chance he would just have to take. He knocked and then, one more time, felt the air was knocked out of his lungs, when Daniella answered. Not only was he relieved her parents did not answer and were nowhere to be seen, but he could not believe the vision standing before him. Daniella's hair was longer, her face smoother and even with the basketball looking stomach, she was still gorgeous. He, awkwardly, put his arms around her and then worried he would hurt the baby. He jumped back and told her she looked beautiful. Daniella simply glowed and invited him in.

The first few minutes were strained and flustered while the two young people tried to acclimate themselves to the fact they were different. They were still teenagers, but they were parents to be. They had created a life that would forever bind them in the one way or the other. Suddenly, both began blabbering and blubbering and then kissing and crying. When they regained some self-control, they sat and David began. He apologized profusely and repetitively and then told Daniella he wanted to be there for her and the baby. She let him know how much he hurt her; how this had really put a wrench in her trust of him and how alone she had felt. She let him know her parents were not being supportive and that if she had not had Summer, she did not know what she would have done. David felt lower than a slithering snake, but it just confirmed for him he had to do what it took to win back Daniella's trust. Relief, like a waterfall, suffused his soul when Daniella told him she forgave him and wanted him in the baby's life.

The young people talked for hours; David was continuously amused and intrigued by Daniella's stomach, as well as the fact, she ate almost nonstop the whole time he was there. David teased her good-naturedly about it, but assured her she was still the most gorgeous girl he knew. They then sobered and discussed how they had to make adult plans now—they were going to have a baby. David told her he would be there from this point on and that his parents would be there for them, too.

CHAPTER EIGHTEEN

The Baby—Parenthood

As Daniella and David tentatively renewed their relationship, David began to settle down. He was now in his senior year of high school and had decided he needed to "get serious". He had played around so much in school previously, it was hard to develop self-discipline for studying, but he was trying to grow up. David had managed to save some of his money from his summer job, especially once he stopped dating a lot of girls. Daniella never expected material things from him, though he liked to give them to her, and so he was able to save.

Though David and Daniella thought their relationship would pick up where they left off, they soon found this was a delusion. Daniella was growing bigger by the day, hormones were fluctuating and she now had serious trust issues with David. David, on the other hand, was still a teenage boy trying to learn how to cope with the reality of pending fatherhood and becoming very frustrated when Daniella would express distrust. He could not comprehend why she could not just let the past stay in the past. Regardless, the young couple really made a concerted effort to correct the mistakes and to prepare for parenthood.

David decided he needed to "be a man" and "do the right thing" so he proposed to Daniella. She, rather hesitantly, accepted, but reminded him he was still a minor. David said this was no problem; he was sure his parents would sign for him to marry. After all, his dad had assured him they would be there for him. Daniella, being eighteen, was not the least concerned about her parents. She felt estranged from them, anyway. Passing in the hallway, exchanging necessary information and being updated to what her current bank balance was, were the primary contact between Daniella and her parents. One thing about the Sanchezs, they always provided financially for their offspring-it was the "right thing" to do.

When Daniella accepted David's proposal, he was ecstatic. He believed this made him a real man and that he was once again, in control. He almost bounced home that night, in his excitement. His parents were not there when he arrived so he went to call Nelson and share his engagement news with him. Before he could dial Nelson's number, however, he heard his mother's car. He decided to tell her first. He was very pleased when he went to the door saw his father's rig pulling into the driveway, too. He would tell them both at the same time.

Mr. & Mrs. O'Brien were giggling like teenagers themselves, when entering the house. Mr. O'Brien had not only surprised David, but his wife, as well. She had not expected him for two more days, so was very happy to see him. After over twenty years of marriage, the O'Briens were still very much in love. David briefly imagined his parents were he and Daniella. He was so overcome with anticipation; he actually hugged his parents. They returned the hug, but wondered what had happened to their teen son that he would display this unexpected show of affection. They soon found out.

David smiled widely and burst out with Daniella and I are getting married". His parents stopped in their tracks and said "what?" He repeated himself and grinned widely. David was completely unprepared to hear both of his parents state unequivocally and almost simultaneously, "no you are not". David's jaw hung slack and his eyes grew wide. He asked, "why not?" His father responded that he was too young and they would not sign. "You said you would do what you could to help me. Besides, you both like Daniella." His parents had him sit and responded that they did indeed care for Daniella. They, also, said they definitely would help the young people out, but not by giving them permission to enter the holy state of matrimony. His mother stated her usual "two wrongs don't make a right". She said they were planning to help take care of the baby, but that David had to stay in school. He said he would and dad stated his usual "many a road has been paved with good intentions". David did not really know nor care what these sayings meant; he just wanted to hear that his parents were signing for him to marry Daniella. The argument went long into the night, but finally, David gave in and said he would wait.

He, adamantly, stated he was going to marry her as soon as he turned eighteen and they could not stop him. They agreed this was true, but ended with one of their other tired old sayings of "we'll cross that bridge when we come to it".

David slept fitfully that night and worried that Daniella would be very upset with him again. The next morning, he awakened red-eyed and exhausted. With dread, he called Daniella and was very surprised at her response. She told him that was okay as long as he was there for her. She admitted she was really frightened to get married anyway. She said having a baby was a little more than she could handle at that time; becoming a wife at the same time was somewhat overwhelming to her. David admitted he had been caught up in the enthusiasm of acting like an adult, but that he too felt some relief.

As time passed, David and Daniella did as well as they could in preparing for parenthood. David went to school and got a part-time job after school. The young people bought necessary items for the baby. Daniella sought advice from David's parents and Summer's mom. Summer's mom got Daniella into Lamaze classes and either Summer and/or David attended with her. Daniella and David resumed a more routine social life with Summer and Nelson. As delivery time drew near, all of the youth became more serious and frightened, but they were a tight knit group and very supportive of each other. David even ceased engaging in juvenile and borderline criminal antics and was becoming more and more responsible.

One Saturday evening, the four teens had been gathered at Summer's home. Daniella was spending the night at Summer's, but she had been grouchy all evening. She snapped everybody's head off, ate without ceasing and would pace and pace throughout the house. David and Nelson decided to leave early and Summer just tried to "be a friend" and let the hurtful comments bounce off of her.

Around ten p.m., Daniella began moaning and sweating and said she could not get comfortable. Finally, Summer called to her mom who came in and took one look at Daniella. She asked some questions about the pain and how they felt, as well as how frequent they were coming. Daniella was in labor. Summer called the O'Brien home and spoke with Mrs. O'Brien. Her mom contacted Daniella's obstetrician and then they left for the hospital. By the time they got there, Daniella was no longer moaning, but howling. Summer felt helpless with fear. Daniella was immediately rolled into the labor room since she was pre-registered at the hospital.

The doctor and the O'Briens arrived about the same time. Dr. Sutton told them she would report to them as soon as she had examined Daniella. She came out within fifteen minutes and inquired who planned to be in the delivery room with them. Mrs. O'Brien and David said they would be there. Summer was trying to call the Sanchezs, but was not being very successful.

Labor was actually fairly short, but Daniella could have sworn it was days long. David could have, too, since Daniella kept screaming at him and then squeezing his hand so hard, he thought it would break. This was very scary. This was nothing like he had thought. When the baby finally arrived, David felt faint and excited. Daniella was just very tired and relieved. When the couple saw the baby, nevertheless, as with new parents, they both decided this was just the most beautiful baby in the world. They cried, they hugged and they stared at the baby in wonderment. Neither had seen such a tiny human being; yet, felt so much love, fear and responsibility for this tiny human. Shaquille, as they named him after David's favorite basketball star, was eight pounds, twelve ounces and twenty-one inches long. Mrs. O'Brien was very amused at the young people as they talked about how small he was and she was thinking "what a huge baby my grandson is".

The Sanchezs actually arrived by the time Daniella delivered. When the baby was in the nursery and everyone, including Summer, her mom, Nelson and the Sanchezs went to view the baby, Daniella's parents actually became overcome with unexpected emotion towards the baby. They felt bad for how they had treated Daniella and wondered if maybe this baby would be the bridge to repairing years of a bad relationship.

By the time David left the hospital, for the second time in his life, he was in love. He was completely in love with his son. What he felt was not unlike what his father had felt seventeen years earlier when he himself, had been born. As he was lying in bed that night, he grinned to himself, just thinking of his son—his own 'little shorty. The heavy, and sometimes unpleasant, responsibility of parenthood had yet to settle on his young shoulders.

David immediately went to the hospital the next morning. He was anxious to see both Daniella and the baby. He wondered if Daniella would now "look like a mom". He had actually spent an inordinate amount of time looking in the mirror at himself this morning. Naively, David had thought he would look different now that he was a dad. When he did not, he wondered if Daniella would look differently. Maybe girls looked different after becoming moms even if boys did not look different as fathers.

Upon arrival to the hospital, David went straight to the nursery. Panic set in when he saw the empty baby bed with his son's name on it. He pounded on the nursery glass until a nurse came out and reprimanded him for knocking on the glass. David quickly mumbled an apology, but asked what happened to the O'Brien baby boy. The nurse recognized new father jitters and calmly placed her hand on his shoulder; suggested he 'breathe' and then assured him the baby was fine. One of the other nurses had simply taken him to another room where she was changing his diaper. David literally slumped in relief. At that moment, he saw two things almost concurrently. The first was the return of his son to the weird little cubicle they kept babies in. The second was a familiar female figure walking in the opposite direction. Surely it was not; it could not be! David blinked to clear his thoughts and eyes and looked again. Sure enough, bouncing down the hallway away from him was Brooklyn. It appeared she had exited Daniella's room.

David would have freaked out if he had known Brooklyn indeed had been with Daniella. She had managed to find out about Daniella, the baby and which room she was in. When she entered the room Daniella had looked up with an anticipate smile, thinking it would be David. Instead, this stranger had walked in, smiled at her, took an uninvited seat and began talking with her as if she knew her.

With a half smile belying the angry tone in her voice, Brooklyn questioned, "You are the mom, huh?" Hesitating and then blinking, Daniella said "huh?" She was taken completely by surprise since she neither knew this person or what she was talking about. Brooklyn responded, "You are the mother of the baby, aren't you?" "What?" Daniella responded, trying to grasp who this person was and what she meant. Brooklyn, rather sarcastically repeated herself slowly, drawing out the words. "Are…you…the…mother…of…the…baby?" Daniella, becoming flustered and angry, responded in the same manner with "what…baby?" Brooklyn, with a heavy and irritated sigh, said "David's baby?" Daniella stared in astonishment and finally said, "How do you know David?" Brooklyn answered with a sly grin, "Girl, you know he is my man! I know you tried to trap him with this baby, but he is my man. He is just spending time with you because of the baby". Daniella's blood boiled and her face flushed bright red, "what?" she asked again. Brooklyn tossed her hair, crossed her legs and said "are you dumb or something? Do you not know any word, but "WHAT"? No wonder David spends his time with me". Daniella shook her head as if to clear it and simply repeated "what?" Daniella thought she must still be feeling the after effects of the anesthesia. Brooklyn just got angry and stomped out of the room, mumbling to herself, "stupid idiot".

Brooklyn never even saw David coming down the hall. As she punched the button in the elevator to the parking garage, she was grinding her teeth and feeling rage. She needed David and Daniella to break up and had thought approaching Daniella would do it. When she started towards her car, she became angrier. She had been forced to park on the top floor of the parking garage and thus, had no cover over her car. As she got into her car, she noted birds had gotten to her car and she mumbled, "stupid birds". She threw open her car door and left it standing open while she dug in her trunk to find some paper towels to clean the hood and windshield of her car. She then threw towels on the ground, got back into her car, still feeling furious. Leaving the garage and getting onto the interstate. Brooklyn heard some fluttering and saw shadows through her rearview mirror. She could not believe it. A bird had gotten into her car. It must have happened while she was cleaning the hood. This startled her so, she failed to notice her car swerving off of the road. Brooklyn hit the guardrail hard. Air bags deployed, banging her in the face and her car was dented and smoking. Brooklyn passed out. Next thing, she knew, she was in an ambulance. She never knew who called the ambulance, but when she came to full consciousness in her hospital room, her rage returned. She was angry with Daniella, the bird and most of all, David. All of this was David's fault.

Meanwhile, David had been standing uncertainly outside Daniella's room. Having seen Brooklyn exited, he was mustering his courage and strength to enter the room. After spending about fifteen minutes, debating what he should do, he became hopeful that maybe Daniella would be sleeping. Peeping into the room, David was sorry to see Daniella staring at the door. When she saw him, she crooked her finger back and forth as if to say, 'get in here'. with dread, David dropped his head inwardly sighed and slowly entered the room.

Daniella, still recovering from her strange visit from the unknown girl, stared at David and asked, "Where have you been? With your little friend?" "Uh, what friend?" David stuttered. "Your little girlfriend that was just here", Daniella responded. David decided to act baffled. "Sweetheart, what are you talking about? Who was just here? You know you are my woman! Are you maybe still drugged? I've been looking at our little shorty". He began going on and on about the baby, trying to change the subject. He had no idea what Brooklyn had said or done and was really afraid to find out. Daniella was not going to be sidetracked by this; she was too tired and furious. She simply said, "David, why don't you leave? We'll talk later". David stuttered, "but, but" as he shifted from foot to foot. Daniella used a few choice words and asked him again to leave. David stared at Daniella for a few minutes, walked slowly to the door, turned and whispered, "I love you". Daniella neither looked up nor responded.

With head hung down and heart feeling loaded down with lead weight, David went backt to look at the baby again and then get on the elevator to leave. He could not believe what was happening. What was Brooklyn up to? He thought they were long over. Whatever had possessed him to ever spend time with that psycho. He mused over this all of the way home.

As soon as he arrived home, the phone was ringing. He hoped it was Daniella and tried to get to the phone before his mom did. When he heard his mom say he was not there (she had not heard him come in), he rushed into the living room where she was. She was hanging up, looked at him as if disappointed; she then shook her head in disbelief and said "I thought you had left that girl alone". David thought to himself, "what now", but he answered with "What girl?" His mother said "Brooklyn. That was her on the phone". Mrs. O'Brien told David Brooklyn had said for him to call her at the hospital. David's heart stopped. His mother went on to say Brooklyn was claiming to be in the hospital and had left her room number. David said, "Mom, I promise I am not with her. I do not know what she is up to, but I am not responsible for anything she is claiming. I am going to go over to Nelson's". Mrs. O'Brien simply tsked, tsked as moms will do and David went to find Nelson. He needed another male with which to talk and his dad would not be home for several days.

Arriving at Nelson's home, David was anxious to see him. Nelson's grandmother told him he was in his room, playing with his Play Station, "as usual", she said with a smile. She sent David on into his room. She was so pleased Nelson had David as his buddy.

Nelson looked up when David came in and simply said "Hi, Davie" as if expecting him. Nelson was leaning back on the bed and David sat down beside him on the bed. Nelson continued playing until he realized David was not talking. Nelson asked "whassa matter with Davie?" David did not immediately respond. Nelson asked, 'can

Nelson help Davie". David shook his head and said only if you can kill her. Nelson, even in his innocence, was so close to David, he immediately knew David had to be talking about that Brooklyn girl. David proceeded to tell Nelson about the events of the afternoon. Nelson responded with "Nelson not like Brooklyn; Nelson like Daniella and Davie like Daniella. What you gonna do Davie?" This innocent response simply validated for David that he did indeed like and love Danielle. He would have to confront Brooklyn and then try straighten this mess out with Daniella. David told Nelson. "You are right. I need to squash this now". David sat in silence a few moments more and then told Nelson, "I am going to the house; I will holler at you later". Nelson, in a way that only the innocent can, said "okay" and resumed his game playing.

David decided he had to be a man and confront Brooklyn. He went to the hospital instead of home and asked for her room number. Brooklyn had been in an accident—this was not another one of her ploys. David felt the familiar tug of pity, but pulled himself together, bit the bullet and told Brooklyn she had to let it go. Brooklyn wailed, but David remained strong. He told her he was sorry how things got so messed up, but he was a father and had to take care of his son. Brooklyn did feel hurt, but she had to admit to herself, she felt some admiration for David, too. After all, she had never known her father and wondered if she would have had a different life if she had. Brooklyn got discharged from the hospital the next day. She had the fleeting thought of stopping by Daniella's room anyway, but decided to leave it alone. Later, at home, she was glad she had when she received a letter in the mail from Jerome. He was getting out in two weeks. She decided to try to let go of her fear and her own need to control and work on the relationship with Jerome. Maybe, just maybe, she and Jerome could have what obviously David and Daniella had.

David was deeply relieved that Brooklyn had not caused a scene in the hospital room. After confronting her and not giving in to her crying, he had gone outside, walked around the hospital in order to gain his composure. He knew he had dealt with Brooklyn, but also realized he was not out of the doghouse with Daniella. He, somehow, would have to explain Brooklyn to Daniella.

Daniella had been emotional all afternoon. This was partly from the aftermath of delivery and partly from the confrontation with the strange girl. David, obviously, knew this girl and she had indicated there was something intimate between the two of them. Daniella had hoped David had changed and that she, he and the baby were going to be a family. She knew they were young and being parents was a heavy responsibility, but she had thought they would be the exception to the norm. Daniella had to admit, if only to herself, that she did not know any teen relationships that had worked. She did not know any girls who had become pregnant who were still with the fathers of their babies. She began to sob quietly. How would she make it on her own with a baby? She had the finances, but what about time, love, knowledge and David? Daniella was so frightened and sobbing so deeply, yet silently, she did not hear the door open. Suddenly, she heard a raspy whisper- "Daniella?" Daniella wiped furiously at her tears, tried to regain her composure subtly and then looked up. There stood David, looking sheepish, staring at her. She wanted to ignore him or to throw him out of the room, but instead she just stared at him and motioned for him to fully enter the room. David ran over, hugged her stiff body and muttered into her hair that he was so, so sorry.

Taking a deep breath, straightening up and forcing himself to look Daniella in the eye, he began to explain about Brooklyn. He told Daniella how he had dated her a few times, but how he never forgot Daniella. He told her how stupid he had felt many times with Brooklyn and how hindsight helped him see how Brooklyn often used him. He told her how he liked her, but did not love her and how most of the time, he simply felt pity for her. Daniella listened quietly, though her heart felt as if it had a knife permanently embedded; yet loose enough to be twisted and turned. She hurt really bad; she felt more betrayal from David. Through this mist of pain, nevertheless, Daniella realized David was telling her this, not to hurt her, but with the intentions of making her realize there was really nothing going on with Brooklyn. Daniella seemed to grow up and mature years beyond her age in that instant. It would take that for her to once again forgive David. In her newfound, albeit fleeting and sporadic maturity, Daniella recognized that David did not understand his dismissal of his relationship with Brooklyn hurt almost as much as his having been with her. He could not understand that he was basically telling her that he had risked their relationship and commitment with something he called "frivolous". How could he throw away their love that easily and lightly? This was the part that hurt, but she decided she had to "let it go". As a mom, she was sure there were much more important things for them to discuss and which needed their focused attention. Having been lost in her swirl of emotions and floundering thoughts, Daniella was unaware David was tensely awaiting her response to his previous monologue. When she noticed his standing there, appearing afflicted by his behaviors, thoughts and emotions, Daniella was freed from the past. She reached out to David, hugged him tightly and asked if he had seen Shaq that afternoon. As tears once again freely flowed down David's cheeks, he had to shrug off the feeling of being a "crybaby" and focus on the fact that Daniella forgave him. He was shaking his head "no" about having not seen Shaq that afternoon, when the hospital door opened again. David tensed, thinking he had not missed the wrath of Brooklyn after all, but then he noticed the wide grin on Daniella's face. He looked again at the door and in walked the nurse with his baby. David stood stock still in awe. This was "his" baby, "his and Daniella's". Maybe, his future was much brighter than he had ever imagined it could be.

CHAPTER NINETEEN

The Last Straw—Drake

Drake stood on top of the twenty-five storied building in a sniper-like stance. With trembling lips and furrowed brow, he trained his rifle on the unsuspecting citizens below. Before pulling the trigger, he was blinded by flashes of his life. He recalled how he and Jonathan used to crouch under their twin beds as their parents fought and screamed in the next room. The very attractive blonde haired, blue-eyed looks of this male belied the torment he daily experienced within his mind.

Wiping sweat from his brow and out of his eyes, Drake could vividly envision himself as a small, scared little boy. Drake never remembered his parents hugging, kissing or even voicing any kind words to each other. He could even remember standing in his crib and hearing the lightening, monster noises coming from the next room. He always thought large, hiking, blue or black or green, fanged monsters would pop into his room, but instead, his mom or dad would walk in, throw him down in the crib and cover him with a shabby blanket. Though he was less than three at the time, he could still recall how it felt and how frightened he was. As Drake grew, the fear never went away. He always felt chilled to the bone and his muscles were always tensed. Drake could not remember life without aching bones, muscles, furrowed brow and fear in his heart.

When Drake was six years old, his parents divorced. His mother took him and his brother and moved from Texas to this small Tennessee town. Drake had hoped life would be better then, but he could not seem to recover from the first five years of his life. Life was peaceful on the outside as far as the physical abuse was concerned, but Drake's mind did not heal. He still remembered seeing his mom with puffed and blackened eyes. He still recalled her being taken away by ambulances and returning home with her arms or legs or even her head in a cast. Drake still remembered being pummeled by his father when his mother would be hospitalized. To this day, when he was frightened, he would crawl into small places and scrunch his six-foot body into a ball and rock back and forth. Drake stayed in the dark as much as possible because he thought this hid him from the world. Drake was often tormented in his dreams by the nightmare life he had lived the first five years of his life. In school, he would stay to himself and the other kids would call him names. Everyone thought he was weird and so did he. His brother seemed to bounce back from the abuse when they moved to Tennessee, but Drake never did.

Drake's mother sporadically tried to understand him and talk with him; she, however, was still so traumatized herself from the abuse she took, she did not do this on a consistent basis. If she had, things may have been different. Drake withdrew more and more. When he was younger, his teachers thought he was shy so they did not intervene. When he was an adolescent, his teachers thought he was being a typical sullen teenager, so they did not question him either. As a young collegiate, there was such a diversity of persons, no one noticed. Throughout all of this, Drake would maintain his grades, keep his clothes neat and clean and respond politely anytime he had no choice but to interact. No one ever knew the daily mental torture Drake suffered.

When in his fourth year of college, Drake met a young lady. She noticed Drake was very quiet, but contributed this to his being the tall, solemn, serious, intellectual type. This, in fact, is what drew her to him and she pursued him. For the first time, Drake felt the stirrings of something more than fear and anxiety. He did not know how to identify this feeling or how to respond to such, but Autumn was so persistent, he finally acquiesced to spending time with her. Autumn was the dominant person in this relationship; the dominance, nevertheless, was not the aggressive, overbearing type. It, instead, was the take charge, confident dominance that Drake needed over himself. Autumn liked being in charge and felt safe with Drake. Guys generally tried to dominate her so Drake was a nice change of pace. The two graduated and Drake entered graduate school. He found, with Autumn, he did not have to crouch in dark corners as much and some of his nightmares dissipated. His mother loved Autumn and approved of the relationship. His brother moved on with life and so Drake turned more and more to Autumn to validate himself as a person.

Since Autumn seemed to care so much for him and she was his only tentative place of security, Drake readily agreed when she wanted to get married. The couple married and Drake thought maybe now he could have life. All went well for a while, but when finances got tight, Autumn became pregnant and miscarried and Drake could not find a job after obtaining his masters in business, stress began to take its toll on Drake. Autumn became withdrawn after her miscarriage and was not as emotionally available to validate Drake's existence. She, as a matter of fact, sought to be comforted and solaced by Drake. When he was unable to provide this since he had never received it himself before meeting her and did not really know how to show support, Autumn became angry. She began raising her voice and withholding love from Drake. All this did was open old wounds and then the nightmares began recurring nightly. They were more intense and Drake could not focus on anything during the day. Soon, he began to have nightmares during the day when he was awake. This eventually led to hallucinations, both auditory and visual. Drake did not know what was happening to him and he began to withdraw from life. Needless to say, this put even more of a strain on the marital relationship. Autumn had returned to work, but was not her old self. She was angry, hurt and feeling burdened by having to "carry" both herself and Drake, financially, socially and emotionally. The day she came home and found Drake crouched under the kitchen counter, rocking and hitting at nothing she could see, she felt she could no longer handle it. Autumn obtained psychiatric help for Drake, but she then moved out and filed for divorce.

Sadly, Drake had never seen fit to share his horrific childhood with Autumn. If he had, she would have gladly helped him get help from the beginning, which could have possibly prevented all of this. Autumn, nonetheless, never knew—she was currently desirous only of getting away from her own personal pain starting anew. Autumn's decision resulted in Drake living in his cold, dark, lonely world of pain, distress, and helplessness. Drake was eventually diagnosed with post-traumatic stress disorder. He qualified and began receiving disability. He then became hermetic and lived for more than three years wrapped in his emotional box of being betrayed by everyone who should have loved and protected him, but did not.

On this fateful day atop the tallest building in town, Drake had all of this pain flash before his eyes and burrowed in his very being. This morning, he had awakened decided he would no longer suffer this pain. Before suicide, however, he needed to show the world what they had done to him, how they had failed him. This is why he was here, with his bag of guns and why David being in the wrong place at the wrong time caused his life to take one of the worst turns ever.

As Drake was sweating, crying and remembering his life, David and Nelson were happily riding the elevator to the top of this same building. Before exiting to the roof of this building, there was a solarium on the twenty-fifth floor. Nelson knew it was there; he had seen pictures and recently he and David had tried to get in to the solarium, but it was already closed when they got there. Earlier today, Nelson had insisted "Davie, Davie, let's go to the 'larium; let's go to the 'larium". Instead of the Arcade that day, David had agreed. Daniella was busy and besides, the boys were growing older and more mature; at least, David was. Nelson, of course, was not maturing as quickly because of developmental delays. David would try to protect and compensate for Nelson's lack. This led them to the Solarium that fateful day.

As the seventeen-year old boys were looking out the windows of the solarium, Nelson spied a brightly colored bag sitting near the ledge of the roof. "Davie, what's that? Let's go see". Before David could respond, Nelson was off and running. By the time David reached him, Nelson had reached the bag and pulled out a rifle. Simultaneously, David noticed the bright orange bag was full of arsenal, heard a gunshot, sirens and commotion behind him. Directly in front of him, Nelson had begun pulling out the various guns and yelling, "wow, wow". Before David could make him put the guns away, he saw police exiting the solarium onto the roof. With the speed of lightening and with the impulse of protective instinct, David grabbed the gun out of Nelson's hands before the uniformed police could see he had them. He was wondering what was happening, but above all, he wanted to make sure Nelson did not get in trouble.

The next few minutes moved in slow motion. Another gunshot could be heard, some of the police were running around the corner of the building, while others ran towards Nelson and David. Shouting shattered the air, guns were drawn and the cold steel of handcuffs was locked onto David's wrists. Nelson was crying, "don't take my Davie; don't hurt my Davie; he not do anything". David overheard a rookie cop asking what Nelson meant while an older police told him "that's the local dummy; ignore him." The next thing David knew he was sitting in the police precinct being illegally questioned while awaiting his parents. He had no idea what had happened to Nelson and was currently more worried about him than he was his own fate. He, therefore, never shared with the police that he had nothing to do with this and had only been trying to protect his friend. He was too afraid it would somehow backfire on Nelson if he did.

Meanwhile, Drake had not successfully shot anyone; had simply misfired. David, as was often his source of information, learned from the news that the young man who was shooting, had been around the corner from them; had, had a breakdown and had been admitted to an inpatient psychiatric institution.

(The Judge)

As David sat in the courtroom, he was sweating with the internal fear he was trying to hide, but actually feeling. He relived his life in mental pictures in the format of a television movie. He wondered what sentence the judge would pass. David realized there were many things he should have been convicted of; yet, the one time he was innocent, he was sitting awaiting the sentence that would determine his immediate future. As he sat nervously waiting and attempting to still his tapping fingers and shaking legs, he looked at the judge and was fairly certain the judge had no idea what it was like to be him. David had heard of Judge Isley before due to some of his peers who had appeared before the judge. He had always felt the judge was too harsh and had no idea what it was like to be a kid.

As Judge Isley was pondering what to do with this young man, he determined to learn more about David and what had possibly led to this. He had often seen this same young man sitting in the courtroom as many of his (David's) school chums had passed through this very courtroom. Judge Isley had always had an instinctive feeling about David, but since until now he had never come through his courtroom as a defendant, he had made an effort to dismiss it. As he looked at David obviously making an attempt to show some bravado, he briefly recalled his own upbringing. As he often had over the years, he uttered a silent prayer of thanks to God that he had the parents and upbringing he did.

Judge Isley, just like David, had made profound decisions, at the tender age of six. Unlike David, however, his parents did not have the stress of making ends meet. Also, unlike David, he did not grow up as an only child and unlike David, his experience led him down a more positive path. The impact on the six year old, however, was just as significant for him as it was for David.

Judge Isley thought about how different his life could have been if it had not been for the patience, understanding and firm hand of his father. He had always been very stubborn and was complaining to his father his very first day of school. He did not want to go and felt there was no reason. In response, instead of his father just saying he had to go, he had instead given him a motivation to go to school. His father had driven him through some of the poorer sections of his hometown and had pointed out the shacks, run down housing projects and broken down vehicles in the yards. He had told him this was a reality for many people and this could easily become Richard's world if he was not careful. Richard was halfheartedly listening to this repetitive lecture from his father. After all, what did his father really know? His father was a prosperous businessman. He owned a dry cleaning business, as well as several rental properties. His mother was a homemaker who seemed to love raising him, along with seven brothers and sisters. She seemed very contented taking care of the house and family. They did not live in this type of run down neighborhood and Richard did not know why his father would even act as if he would have to one day. What did going to school have to do with this? He later learned the point of this little excursion was to teach him the importance of education and being able to make informed and better choices.

At the age of six, however, this meant nothing to him. Up to this point in his young life, Richard had known only wealth and comfort. Why his family lived in a five bedroom, three-level home and had two nice automobiles. In addition to the material comforts of life, Richard, unlike many of not only his African American peers, but most children in that era, had the privilege of enjoying two week annual family vacations. His family would also frequently visit his paternal grandparents in Alabama; these grandparents lacked for nothing either. In fact, they had succeeded enough to buy and live on a twelve-acre farm. At the time, nevertheless, Richard was way too young to understand this being the exception to the rule for most people, especially people of color.

As Richard entered school and naturally grew older, however, he never forgot the ride he had taken with his dad that day, on his very first day of school. He had only been six then and had acted as if he was not really listening, but it had still had a major impact in his life. He never forgot what he had seen and began to look at what he and his family had differently. This became even more significant as he noticed children in his first grade that did not dress as nice as him; their parents did not always pick them up from school in nice cars and many had to walk or ride busses home. Richard became a little more observant and was receptive to his parent's insistence that he study. This resulted in his actually excelling in school and eventually learning to enjoy it.

The summer after high school graduation and before entering Moore House College in Atlanta where he planned to pursue higher education, Richard visited with his paternal grandparents again. Feeling contented with his life and contemplating the excitement of entering school and becoming one of the few Black CPA's, at the time, Richard decided to take his morning routine jog before joining his grandparents for breakfast.

During his jog, Richard had the intense impression of being watched and at one point, thought he actually heard his name being called. Initially he thought it was his grandfather calling, then he thought he was too deep in thought, but then suddenly he recalled early Sunday School lessons he had learned as a child. His parents being very religious persons, Richard had been reared in church and had a natural faith in God. He recalled the story of Sampson and wondered if God was maybe calling to him. He took a moment for silent reflection and automatically uttered a prayer heavenward that if this was indeed God, to make it clear. Within moments, Richard had the deepest conviction and sudden clarity that he might be of more benefit in law than the almost purely money making business of being a CPA. Richard's father had always encouraged his children to be honest, caring, grateful for what they had, and to share with those in need. Law might be the answer.

Again, Richard heard his name, but this time it was his grandfather. His grandfather, teasingly, jousted with him, and then said "Boy, I've been looking for you. Mother has breakfast on the table and she won't let me eat until you come back. Let's go!!" Richard playfully punched his grandfather in the arm and then shared his very recent experience. His grandfather validated for him he should be very attuned to the spiritual and take it into account. Richard had done just this and had changed his major to law before he even entered school. It did, however, change which school he felt he needed to attend. He called his father about this, who gave him full support.

After visiting with the grandparents and then returning home, he began applying for different colleges, including Yale and Harvard. He knew his grades would meet their stringent criteria, despite the lateness of application and racial and social climate. To alleviate some of the burden of expense of attending one of these colleges, Richard wanted to apply for academic scholarships. He had become very cognizant of his fortune and wanted to take some responsibility for his own choices. He was shocked therefore, when his father said there was no need. His father had suggested scholarship monies should be left for those who were in dire need of the help.

Judge Richard Isley recalled his gratitude and delight when he was accepted at Harvard University. He, also, recalled the next four years proving to be some of the most challenging he had ever experienced in his young life. So much was changing in America. Not only was school changing, but the political and social environments of the world, were as well. The civil rights movement was in full swing, Vietnam was the political issue and the nuclear family was becoming less important. Richard, thus, was dealing with keeping his grades up, obstacles of racism in a predominantly white university and a general change in America's value system about the family. Richard still managed to graduate in the late sixties in the top twenty percent of his class.

From that point on, everything fell into place, including his obtaining a position at a very prestigious firm via the help of God, he felt. Richard remained faithful to his spiritual beliefs. He always prayed for wisdom before arguing each case. His success rate was astonishing—out of the 568 cases he argued, he only lost 15.

It was in the early nineties when Richard Isley, at the age of 56, decided to leave the law firm and run for position of judge. Due to Richard remaining true to his values and spiritual beliefs, he became painfully aware of the mistreatment by the unfair rulings of judges and thought he might be useful in that position. He felt he was being spiritually prompted once again. Richard was not egotistical, but because of instilled values and mores, truly saw people as people and not as cases. It was this very reason he was so very interested in the young people who came through his courtroom. He, thus, was genuinely interested in young David at this time and wanted to be sure he made a wise decision. He based many of his decisions on the biblical story of when Solomon had to pass judgment regarding who was really the mother of a baby. Solomon, too, had been a man who had prayed for wisdom, was a just judge and had, as blessings from God, accumulated much material wealth. This only further validated for Richard that God had a hand in placing him here and he took it seriously.

Over the years, he earned the reputation of being tough, but fair. He was often given the nickname of the "Tough Love Judge" by peers and colleagues. David had viewed him only as "tough" and did not and could not know how Judge Isley had arrived at this point in his life. He did not know that he was really very interested in making a decision regarding David that would be in the best interest of him despite David's history with trouble.

Keeping consistent with his deep convictions, Judge Isley decided David might need a psychological profile done. This led him to assigning Dr. James Watkins to the case of David O'Brien.

CHAPTER TWENTY

The Counselor—David

Since David was being mute about why he had the guns, his court appointed attorney decided he could do nothing for him. It seemed he had been suspected of involvement in many incidents and adolescent pranks not provable. This crime of gun possession, however, was serious. This was the primary reason Judge Isley was so determined to have David evaluated. He really believed there was more to this young man and his behavior than what met the naked eye.

Not unlike his familiarity with Judge Isley, David had also heard of Dr. Watkins. The community was often atwitter about the good doctor. David, however, did not believe in counseling. Seeing him as opposed to going directly to jail and do not pass go; do not collect $200, though he was relieved for the reprieve—even if it meant seeing a shrink.

(Dr. James Watkins)

In the spring of 1959 in Tokyo, Japan, the family of Colonel James Lewis Watkins II, were thrilled to be welcoming the new addition to their family, James Lewis Watkins, III. Overjoyed at the birth of this third generation James Watkins, the U.S. Air Force Colonel and the very tired, but excited Miyoshi, were basking in their love now being sealed in the form of their new son. They had already had a baby daughter a year earlier, but this was the first male offspring and one who would carry on the family name.

Colonel and Mrs. Watkins loved each other and had from the moment they met on a blind double date with the colonel's best friend. The colonel always described their first meeting as being "love at first sight". Not unlike David's father's response to David's mother, Dr. Watkins' father had been struck by the beauty of his mother. He thought she was like a lovely flower… she was sooo beautiful!!! Also like David's parents, the good doctor's parents had quickly become engaged in a serious relationship and married within seven months of dating. Whereas David's parents had the obstacle of distance, Dr. Watkins' parents had to deal with racial and cultural issues. Here this very brave couple, one American Caucasian and the other Japanese took on the world together in the early fifties due to such love and allegiance for and to each other.

James L. Watkins, III was quite a long name for such a small child so he was quickly nicknamed "JJ" by the general world. His father, however, being a career military person referred to him as "little soldier". David would have felt smug in his assumed assessment of the doctor if he had known this doctor indeed did not suffer the feeling of being invisible or unimportant in his early life. To him, it would have proven the doctor could not possibly know anything about him. His assessment that the doctor had no problems would soon be disproved in a way David would never have imagined.

Having inherited his father's dark curly hair and bright blue eyes and his mother's Asian looks, JJ was a very handsome child. According to his sister, Cho, not only did JJ have the looks and intelligence, he was the apple of his father's eyes. She had once shared how because JJ, by the time he was four, had called his father "the colonel", his father had run with it and insisted everyone else do the same. Even in the present time, the elder Colonel Watkins still was referred to as "the colonel" by family, friends and associates—all because of Dr. Watkins This would have frustrated David even more if he had known because it would have appeared to him that Dr. Watkins got what David had always wanted just by nature of being born.

Whereas David had at least had the stability of living in one geographical area all of his life, the Watkins family had frequently relocated since they were a military family. Most of their assigned stations, however, had been outside the U.S.; in addition, the elder colonel had been an only child and both of his parents were dead; it was years, therefore, before the family actually set foot in the United States. This, nevertheless, still worked to the positive for the Watkins children. Being "military brats" as well as being the product of a bi-racial couple, the children had exposure to all sorts of people. Playmates and school friends consisted of African Americans, Caucasians, Hispanics, and of course, Asians. JJ and his sister, thus, learned manners, consideration of others and to be nonjudgmental of differences in people. This would serve well in his future profession of psychologist.

When the colonel retired from the Air force in the seventies, the family relocated to the United States and settled in the colonel's small hometown in Tennessee- the same town in which David and his father had both been born and raised. The family adjusted quickly and being a child at the time, James Watkins and his sister were thrilled to be able to go to concerts by everyone from the Osmonds to KISS. Again, David would have been infuriated to know of these privileges falling into the doctor's lap. After all, he had often "had to steal" (as he still justified it) to have what he considered the basics, liked "brand name clothing".

With his father now retired from the military and the family being settled in one place, the future doctor was able to actually develop lasting relationships; his grades, which had always been good (B's) were now in the ranks of excellence (straight A's). He joined social and athletic groups. In spite of privileges, James the third, not unlike Judge Isley had early on in life, had and expressed a burning desire to help people. By the age of fourteen, he knew he wanted to be a psychologist, primarily dealing with adolescents. Now with this stability, he felt he could begin working towards his dreams of becoming psychologist. Needless to reiterate, the doc had indeed, achieved his goals and this is how he had become involved in the life of David O'Brien. He was thrilled to be assigned to David's case because he always felt a deep sense of satisfaction and contentment when he worked with troubled young people. They often came in with dejected looks and downcast eyes, but after a few sessions, would walk out with heads held high, a lilt in their voices and a bounce in their steps.

After completing the evaluation of David, Dr. Watkins was recalling details of his own life. Coming to the U.S. had helped Dr. Watkins achieve all of his goals. He had met a beautiful African American woman in his first year at college. Since he himself was bi-racial, someone of a different race did not bother him, but he had worried that Lynne would not be able to handle his heritage. It was with relief, joy and happiness, therefore, when he learned that she had fallen in love with him. The doc recalled the joy of realizing his dream of becoming a psychologist and his wife, Lynne, had realized her dream of opening her own beauty salon. Born to their union were two gorgeous, intelligent and fun loving children. Dr. Watkins, it seemed really had the life David imagined he did. Ironically, this mixed heritage couple had achieved the "American Dream"—two professionals, the big house, the expensive cars, social club memberships and a male and female child. Dr. Watkins, however, had learned of a situation this afternoon that would result in his making one final significant decision about his life.

During his initial venture into his field, Dr. Watkins would feel excited about work everyday and hurry home to share the day's adventures with Lynne. She would, also, share her day, but of course, he could not share as much as she did because his work was of a more confidential nature. The whole family would chatter incessantly when at home together in the evenings. Dinnertime at the Watkins house was almost a party with all of the excitement, talking and sharing. Once the children were engaged in their respective nightly activities, Lynne and JJ could then spend time alone. This was JJ's favorite time of day. He was so in love with his wife! He thanked God on a daily basis for her for he felt he had to be the luckiest man alive. He had been given the privilege of having fantastic parents, a wonderful childhood and now an incomparable family of his own.

JJ would spend hours immersed in his happiness. During breaks at work, he would muse over his life and if opportunity presented, call Lynne at work. She could not always talk from the noisy bustle of her hair salon, but when she could, JJ would declare the heavens had sent him an angel time and time again. Though he loved his work, it was his family that was priority for him. He loved his children with all of his being; however, much of that all encompassing love was due to the children being a part of him and his lovely, desirable wife.

Female co-workers would often flirt with JJ and though he was kind to them, anyone who knew him, knew his one love interest was with Lynne. The office gossip was often centered on how fortunate Lynne was to have a husband like Dr. Watkins. Many females wondered how to get their partners to feel and act towards them as Dr. Watkins did about his wife. There was much harmless envy in the atmosphere for when they actually met Mrs.

Watkins, they too loved her. She was everything Dr. Watkins described—beautiful, cultured and appeared to be adoring of her husband.

The co-workers knew when to back off; clients were a different story. One of the hazards of being a successful psychologist was that clients tended to engage in transference and could develop some fairly serious infatuations. Though Dr. Watkins preferred working with adolescents, he also did counseling with adults. Everyone loved him. These were the accolades David had always heard about Dr. Watkins and before actually being evaluated and witnessing what the big fuss was all about, David had felt irritated about this attention he got. To be expected in this profession, however, his female adult clients often experienced classic transference. They often believed they were in love with Dr. Watkins and would do everything possible to seduce him into relationships with them. Dr. Watkins, however, being the professional he was and being so in love with his wife, had no problems maintaining professionalism. Never tempted by these clients and having an understanding wife, it did not overly concern him when someone would inevitably manage to get his home phone number or home address. They would then call "in crises" or cruise by his home. Lynne would actually laugh at some these stunts and Dr. Watkins would tactfully address the issues within the confines of the sterile counseling office. This family, just as David had imagined, seemed to have it all—a secure marriage, happy children and ideal careers.

Sitting here reviewing his initial impressions of the good doctor and how the evaluation actually was okay with him, David felt a little stirring of hope. While awaiting what his final outcome would be, David recalled how surprised he had been when he was able to open up to Dr. Watkins about many things. He had shared much of how he had felt all of his life, his friendship with Nelson and his fear for the future. It had actually been all right despite the fact that he was still in this place. Whether he was set free or was sent to juvenile for a period of time, David hoped he would get to see more of Dr. Watkins.

Before being escorted back to the courtroom for the final judgment, David had thought long and hard about the doctor. For once in his life, he thought maybe the doctor was okay even if he did 'have it all'. With his back to the television, which was turned down low, David neither saw the picture nor heard the news item of Dr. James Watkins III. After evaluating David, the good doctor had written up his assessment of the situation, had faxed it to the judge and had then placed a .38 in his mouth and pulled the trigger. Unbeknownst to David, while he was being evaluated, Mrs. Lynne Watkins and her lover were lying in a pool of blood where Dr. Watkins had shot them before seeing David.

Right before David was due to come in for his evaluation, Dr. Watkins realized he had left some necessary assessment tools at home. He had cheerfully gone home, hoping to maybe have a few minutes with his wife. Upon arrival, he noted a strange car in the drive, but dismissed it as probably one of her employees. It actually was one of her employees, but a very intimate one. James found his wife entwined in the arms of one of her beauty salon stylists in their bed. It seems this employee had actually been a high school sweetheart of his wife's. Recently, when she was advertising for hair stylists at her shop, he had appeared on her doorstep, not knowing she was the employer. He was hired and as time passed, they knew old feelings had not ever died. Working in close proximity only refueled the embers of their love. Mrs. Watkins truly loved her husband, but could not resist the charms of her first love. They had started a private affair. She knew James had that evaluation that afternoon so they had risked meeting at their home—a fatal mistake.

When Dr. Watkins saw the love of his life in another man's arms, he simply "reacted". He grabbed the .38 special from the drawer of the hallway table and began firing shots until there were none left to fire. Immediately coming to his senses and regretting his actions, a single tear dropped down his face as he turned and walked out the door. Dr. Watkins went back to work, completed David's evaluation, faxed the results and sent his secretary home. He then made that most significant final decision and took his own life. Later that evening, the building security was dumbfounded and grieved to find the beloved Dr. Watkins dead in his office. Both community leaders and co-workers were even more shocked and grieved when police found his wife and her lover dead at the Watkins home. Having gone with the dubious task of telling Mrs. Watkins about her husband's suicide, they found they had an even harder task of telling the Watkins children about the deaths of both of their parents.

Not only was David unaware of this, he would never know this action on the part of the psychologist, legally could have rendered his findings invalid. Fortunately, his findings were not refuted. If they had have been, David's future may have taken an even more treacherous turn.

CHAPTER TWENTY-ONE

The Verdict

While David was sitting hopefully that he would get to work through issues with Dr. Watkins, the news reporter was telling the story of the Murder-Suicide incident that had occurred that very afternoon.

(Trial)

After receiving the report on David, a hearing was set. Three weeks later, the day so many people dreaded had arrived. Now, David, Nelson, Daniella, Summer, Rebecca and John all sat in the courtroom, each experiencing his own private thoughts and emotions.

(Rebecca)

As Rebecca sat in the courtroom, awaiting the judge's entry and watching the back of her beloved son's head, she was having memories flood her thought processes. When David was initially arrested, they had detained him overnight before releasing him on bail. She had gone to see him immediately. When they had taken her in that cold cinderblock room with a glass separating her from her baby, she had been catapulted back to his toddler years. The glass had jolted one memory in particular. This memory had brought bittersweet thoughts and feelings.

When David had been about eighteen months old, the family had gone to Oregon to her mom's home for Thanksgiving. Her mother had a glass top dining room table. The table was just high enough for David to stand under. She slightly giggled to herself even as tears filled her eyes as she recalled David toddling underneath the table repetitively that day. What had been so amusing was he knew how to get under the table, but when he would get there, would not know how to get out. David would stand under the table, look up through the glass, not knowing how to reach his parents. He would cry and cry until someone reached underneath and pulled him out. Awaiting her son to come out to see her that day in detention, Rebecca's heart almost literally bled as she saw the tears in his eyes behind the glass, but this time she could not rescue him.

Rebecca knew David had gotten into several antics over the years. She had needed to talk with schoolteachers and principals; had received phone calls from police who were personal friends and had repetitively reprimanded and punished David. She, however, never thought it would come to this. In addition, within her heart of hearts, she knew David was not being fully forthcoming. She sensed he was hiding something and though she could not prove it, she just knew it had something to do with his feeling of responsibility and loyalty to Nelson.

(John)

John O'Brien sat stock still as he was consumed by his own thoughts and emotions. He constantly cleared his throat, as if it was irritated; in reality, tears were clogging his throat, but he was determined to not shed them. After all, nothing had yet been determined in David's case. John was desperately grasping to the fact that his son was still a minor, barely at the age of seventeen, but still a minor.

Seventeen years! It had been seventeen years ago when John had heard his only son's lusty cry and his dreams had swelled him with pride. He had hoped David would be following in the family footsteps of over the road driving and eventually, owning the truck company John had always desired. As this dream scattered towards the recesses of his mind, the nightmare in which they were all living, seemed to blow up out of proportion.

John was not an uncaring, neglectful father. He, in fact, had tried to provide well for his family and be there for his son. He knew what it was like to be a Black male in America. Times had changed and progress had occurred, but not enough so for John to feel any real hope and comfort about his son's future—not even with a Black judge in control. Mr. O'Brien had been aware of the antics in which David had often been involved. He and Rebecca had often talked and he himself had frequently lectured and administered discipline to his son. He now wondered if it had not been enough. He was concerned he had overlooked something. He even berated himself that he had not taken the previous antics serious enough—deep inside, he had always felt it was a passing phase and a way for David to exert the independence he had always so obviously craved and desired.

John was mentally doubled over in pain, a pain filled with sorrow, regret, fear and guilt. He silently sent a prayer towards heaven that his son would be let off and if not, that they all would be able to handle whatever the outcome.

(Nelson)

Nelson was rocking back and forth as he often did when trying to calm himself. Nelson did not understand why they were here. He knew Davie had not done anything wrong. He had tried to tell everyone this over and over. Why was no one listening?

Nelson dropped within himself in his own private hell. By now, Nelson knew he was different; he did not know what the delays were or even that they were delays—he just knew he was different. Many people still looked at him weird; would ask why he rocked so much and why he talked like he did. Davie and his other friends however did not mistreat Nelson. Nelson's thoughts were processing,

"Davie loved Nelson. Nelson loved Davie. Summer and Daniella were his friends. Daniella and Summer believed Nelson when he said Davie did not do it. Why didn't the police believe him? Why did nobody listen to and trust him like Davie, Summer and Daniella?" Nelson inwardly groaned as his rocking increased. "What would Nelson do without Davie? What was the judge going to do with Davie?" People kept saying Davie might have to go away. "Where would Davie go? Would he be mad at Nelson? Would he forget Nelson?" As the thoughts got sadder and the fear got stronger, a moan, almost like that of a wounded animal, escaped Nelson's lips.

(Summer)

When Summer first heard the animal-like sounds, it had jolted her out of her own thoughts. She then realized it was Nelson and moved closer to him to comfort him. As she put her arms around him and laid his head on her shoulder, her own lips trembled.

With the exception of the trembling lips and sad eyes, the outside observer would never know Summer was the least bit affected by this situation. With her mom being a social worker, Summer had often been exposed to traumatic situations in the lives of others. She had even sat in the courtroom many times while her mom was there to support a client.

Though she always felt bad for people, it was such a part of life for her; she usually was able to handle it. This, however, was different.

David was a friend to Summer. She, however, felt the deeply gripping sadness because of Nelson and Daniella. She could feel Nelson shaking and she had witnessed so many persons being mean to Nelson, she worried what would happen to him should David be incarcerated. She placed a reminder in her subconscious to not lose touch with Nelson if David went away.

The primary worry for Summer was Daniella. Daniella was her best friend. She had already been through so much pain with her parents, her own upbringing, a pregnancy and delivery and the brief period when David deserted her. Summer knew Daniella was strong, but she was a mom now and she really loved and needed David. Summer felt that despite the outside strength Daniella had always shown, she was actually more fragile inside than anyone knew. She was hoping, hoping, David would just get probation. She had seen this happen with kids before, so it was possible. Besides, David had often been in trouble in the past, but he always managed to survive. Summer let her natural optimism peek out from behind the curtain of empathy for David and her friends.

(Daniella)

It felt so cold in here. The walls seemed to be closing in on the room. The straight, hard-backed chairs seemed to be mocking the potential for happiness. Nothing good could come out of this room. The spidery, multiplying fingers of the cold crawled all over Daniella; yet, she felt hot and faint. She just knew she was going to vomit right there. What was that animal moaning? Why were the sounds in here so loud and at the same time so distant? Why was her face and blouse so wet? Daniella had no idea how many tears she had and was shedding even as she sat there. Mrs. O'Brien kept handing her tissue, which Daniella simply held in her left hand. Summer kept patting her right hand with her left one, while holding on to Nelson with her right hand. Daniella wanted to stand up and scream. Maybe, if she did, this nightmare would end. After all, she and David could not be separated again. He was Shaq's father and he loved her. They had already been through their separation. That had to be what was happening—a nightmare! She was having that recurring dream she used to have when she and David were broken up. She just needed to wake up. If she could just stand up, she would wake up. Just as this thought and action were forming, she heard "All rise". Yes, this was what she needed to do, "rise". Daniella was so disoriented and distressed, she had not yet realized this was not a dream; the bailiff was asking everyone to rise as Judge Isley was entering the courtroom. The judge who would just in moments, share with everyone present, his decision about David's immediate future.

(The Final Curtain)

Slumped, both emotionally and physically, David nervously awaited his fate. He had been so certain Dr. Watkins was going to be his new release on life; but then, he never heard back from the good doctor. David never knew of the suicide for no one had shared this information with him. All he had learned was that the results had come in and now here he was back in court.

As he had reflected on many of the adult lives, which had touched his, David wondered, "Was no one happy in this life? Was there even a need to try? Judge Isley was entering the courtroom and David figured his life had ended. Memories of the past and the present swirled inside David's mind in a way that made one indecipherable from the other. While sitting here, he had recalled so many of the details of his life. Young David had lived more and experienced more in his short seventeen years than many persons did who lived to be eighty. David had made poor decisions, had matured in many ways beyond his years, was a new daddy and now was facing incarceration. He rued the day he was six. He had made such a desperate decision at an age when he should not have even been thinking such thoughts. He regretted how at the age of six, he was having thoughts and making decisions that should just now, by all rights, be occurring in his life. He now realized how childish he was when he had thought he was invisible, invincible and powerful. David had been so young and now here he sat, awaiting judgment of his future.

Suddenly, David heard the bailiffs booming voice, stating "All Rise! The honorable Judge Richard Isley presiding". The time had come. Judge Isley went on and on about something David never heard. He was interested only in the verdict-not how he had arrived at this verdict. His attorney motioned for him to rise and stand attention. David almost fainted when the judge ordered him to one year of juvenile and then pending behavior and progress, a potential sentence of three years in prison after he reached eighteen. David heard a muffled cry, turned around and noted his parents, Daniella and Nelson all shedding tears like a faucet. He wanted to comfort and be comforted by them, but that was not an option. As the guards handcuffed him, David dropped his head and shuffled out the courtroom door.

AFTERWORD

As is often quoted by an esteemed friend and colleague, "all human behavior is purposeful". The reasoning may be indecipherable to the naked eye of observers, but the outward manifestation is simply a response to the inward turmoil. Different persons may choose different ways of coping with their troubles, confusions, pains, desires and even happiness. Sometimes, as in the case of David, self-destruction is the chosen path. Unfortunately, this path often has dire consequences not only for the one engaging in such behaviors, but for those with whom he/she has contact/influence as well. Innocent lives are often impacted by the behaviors of others. Ordinary victims have options in which to respond to life's circumstances. Self-destruction, hurting others, remaining victimized or being motivated to aspire to greatness and/or positive change are all individual choices. Though it is necessary that there are consequences for behaviors, it is also necessary to withhold judgment less the victims and victimizers be we.

ABOUT THE AUTHOR

Delrick J. Johnson is a first time author who was born in Tennessee. At the age of twenty, he served in the Armed Forces (Army). Currently working for the E.I. du Pont Nemours and Company, he is the father of two teenaged children. Presently, Mr. Johnson resides in Murfreesboro, Tennessee. Inspired by ordinary people, he endeavored to co-author this novel.

Lisa (Britton) Keith, also a native of Tennessee, is a mother of one and grandmother of one. A bachelor's level social worker, Ms. Keith collaborated with Mr. Johnson to produce this first novel. Having spent the past two decades, working with both the severely and persistently mentally ill and alleged batterers of domestic violence, Ms. Keith believes there are more victims in the world than meets the naked eye. This was part of the inspiration for this novel.